MINE IN HELL

MINE IN HELL

MINE IN HELL

THE REJECTED MATE SERIES

G. BAILEY

SCARLETT SNOW

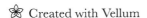 Created with Vellum

DESCRIPTION

Now the world knows who I am.

I'm the first female alpha in history and every pack leader out there wants to claim me as their mate.

Including the Stormfire alpha who sent my life into a spiral after rejecting me.

While he and the others fight for the right to possess me, a new Demon Trial is created in honor of the Crescent Mother, and this time, I'm the prize.

Or so they all believe.

I'll stop at nothing to reclaim my freedom, even if it means entering the trials myself, where the only way out is death.

But I don't plan on dying.

I plan on *winning*.

Then I'm going to make each of the alphas pay for what they did to me.

18+ Dark reverse harem romance full of a sassy and sarcastic heroine who finds her match.

PROLOGUE

*T*he waves crashing over the rocks in the distance pound through my ears like the drums of war. And yet, as quickly as one can seize the life of their foe, a calm silence stretches over the shoreline like a sigh breathed across the ocean.

She's here.

I continue downwind until I emerge through the clearing hidden in the trees. There I locate my belongings buried in a hatch in the ground. I shift into my male form and pull on a pair of jeans. White sand crumbles beneath my feet as I step out onto the beach and make my way to the shoreline.

What appears at first to be a silver mirage is actually the silhouette of an old friend of mine.

"Your Highness," I say, inclining my head and grinning with light-hearted humour. "I did not think you would answer my call tonight."

Eulah clicks her tongue and walks gracefully across the water, the surface rippling with each step. "There is nothing more my brother can do to me that would be worse than the punishment I'm already serving just for threatening his bastard claim to the Dark Fae throne. This night is my freedom to swim, even if I can't go far out to sea or shift." She turns to me, her pale skin glowing like the coronas of the moon. "Now, tell me what is so urgent. You look troubled, Lyulf."

I grunt at that and drag a hand through my hair. "Troubled is one way to put it. Barely slept these past months."

"Then speak of it, my friend, for we both know I am bound to the sea when there is a full moon, and the tide is already fast approaching. What troubles you? Is it your pack?"

I shake my head with a grunt. "Not this time... It's a faceless she-wolf who calls to me at night and only I can hear her."

Eulah narrows her eyes. "You say that she is faceless?" I incline my head, to which Eulah frowns harder at and taps her lips in contemplation. "I see. The gods rarely conceal one's identity from those who should see it." She waves her hand in a slow, circular motion, and gathers water magically into the air. "Let me see what they are trying to tell you."

Magic seeps from her palm and morphs the liquid into four dimensional figures that, at first, are completely transparent and indecipherable to my unseeing eye. But then they change into a deep crimson that splits across the sky, briefly blinding me. It takes several attempts to acclimate my sight again. Even then, the images are still indecipherable. Just a bunch of shapeless figures hanging in the night air.

Eulah lifts her other hand and draws more water from the surface. This time, I am able to make sense of it. The liquid trickles into the image of an enormous tree, one I know all too well, except the *Tree of Ignis* is not as I recall.

Its flames are dying.

From the root all the way to the leaves, an icy shadow sins into the wood and freezes everything in its path. The instant it reaches the portal at the base of the tree, a blast of energy knocks me several feet back, forcing me to dig my boots into the sand and protect my gaze with the back of my hand.

"Eulah, what do you see?!" I call out.

"Death," comes her reply, "and fire. You are in grave danger, my friend."

I chuckle at that. "When am I not in danger, Eulah?"

But the fae, intent on the vision, shakes her head. "Not like this. It is unlike anything I have ever foreseen. So much chaos. So much unnecessary bloodshed." She takes out a deep, shuddering breath. "And it is the faceless one who causes it."

I follow her line of sight and my pulse accelerates when I see what rests on top of the tree. Impaled on the highest branch of all is my corpse. Every muscle in my body tenses, and I swallow, the action unusually difficult.

"Now, I may not possess the ability of foresight," I say, my voice almost a whisper, "but I know a bad omen when I see one. What is the meaning of this?"

Eulah jolts as if dragged back to the present. Blinking at me with a slightly dazed expression, she turns back to the tree. "I am afraid the meaning is clear, my old friend." She moves to study the vision more closely. "This she-wolf who calls to you will be your undoing. She is an alpha, like you, but also an unhallowed born. Many seek to destroy her. Perhaps it is they who bring death and fire to our lands instead of her."

I drag my brows together in contemplation. "So the she-wolf who's been haunting my dreams is an alpha? Why would I risk my life for her? Even a female alpha is not worth leaving my pack bereft of theirs."

Yet as I say the words, I cannot deny how vastly my curiosity has been piqued. There has never been an alpha she-wolf before. Ever. Not as far as I recall, anyway, and I've been around a long fucking time. However, a prophet did once say that a female alpha would destroy our world. I just assumed he was a sexist bastard, and I'd given him a black eye for it too.

But a female alpha… she could be powerful indeed.

"You will not only risk your life," Eulah says, "you will sacrifice it."

I breathe quickly through my nose. "You know, I did gather as much. My impaled corpse was a bit of a giveaway." I drag a hand through my hair and look up at my corpse. "Who is this female I'm to sacrifice my life for?"

In my peripheral, Eulah looks at me. "She is the one you choose to be your mate."

Now it's my turn to stare off into space. Did she just say…

"Well, fuck me," I mutter, crossing my arms again. "That sure as fuck explains things."

Despite the severity of the vision, I laugh. This is downright hilarious. For months now this strange female has haunted my every waking moment. Her howls have carried to me long throughout the night, but I never understood why. It's because she's my mate and her wolf has been calling out for my protection. A strange, urgent need to give that to her consumes me.

"This death and ruin you speak of," I say, glancing back at my friend. "Can it be prevented?"

She gives a slow shake of her head. "It is unclear. Soon, the faceless one will learn of a deep betrayal that will almost destroy her. She will be driven into the Inner City of Hell. You must go to her as soon as she arrives there." Eulah lifts her gaze from the water to look intently at me. "But be warned that if you do, there may be no coming back." Once more the fae looks up at my corpse. "It is not only your death the gods foresee but that of many others. So much bloodshed..."

I harden my features in a determined scowl. I've waited a long time for my mate. Only death itself will keep me from her.

And now that I know the faceless is mine, I won't stop until I've claimed her as my mate.

I'm the first female alpha in all of history.

As I wake up slowly, the thought screams over and over in my mind until it's all I can think about. I feel my wolf curled around my soul, the truth to the words so clear in her mind and so foreign in my own. For a reason only the Mother knows, I was born to a life that would never be easy, and I was blessed with a simple childhood thanks to my mum. I wish she were here so I could thank her for everything she did for me, because it all makes so much sense to me now.

She saved me a million times over, and I never knew it.

"Her arm was broken in several places, alpha, but I've fixed everything else that was life threatening. The young wolf will heal in time, but she'll be sore and tired for a few days at least," I hear an unfamiliar, deep male voice say, feeling his presence nearby. He smells like saltwater, just like someone else in the room, now that he isn't hiding who he is. My body is extremely sore, that's an understatement, and I hardly want to open my eyes. I can still scent my own blood and Alaric's in the room, reminding me of everything that happened. Rizor beating me, the level five demon hunt gone wrong. Dove betraying me. I don't want to face the world quite yet, but I'm aware I need to. Caspian was in danger and Ez was fighting his father, the alpha. They could both be dead, even if I don't want to believe it. "Now let me examine that shoulder of yours."

"I'm fine," Alaric—no, Alpha Lyulf of Rivermare —growls back.

"But alpha—"

"Very well," he agrees, and I hear the sound of fabric ripping as I blink my eyes open, staring up at the clear blue sky above me. The sun shines down on me, keeping me warm as my body floats in some kind of warm water. My head is resting on something soft, half in and out of the water, but the rest of me is under, and I smell sea salt in the air as well as their scent. It's not an unpleasant scent, but it means I'm in the Rivermare pack.

Even with the blistering sun shining on me, it's cold. Well, colder than hell. The last month feels like nothing more than a terrible nightmare, like if I close my eyes, then it will all go away. But it doesn't and it won't.

I have to face the world because my mum didn't raise a quitter. Every little piece of advice and guidance she gave me as I grew up makes so much sense to me now. She was shaping me into a leader, an alpha, shaping the core of who I was born to be.

And a female alpha doesn't rest, scared to face the truth of the world.

I reach out, my icy hands finding ledges at my side and I use them to sit up, letting water drip down my body—which is covered with a dark blue, thick fabric shaped into a dress and tied at my shoulders. My red hair falls down to my waist, and I meet Alaric's eyes first as he sits in the same pool of water opposite me.

The pool is small, cosy even, reminding me of the onsen springs in Japan: the first time I really felt something for Alaric. But it had all been one giant pretence. A lie. I look up at the arched circle of stone around us, the lack of roof to the room, but there is nothing more to look at. Behind Alaric is a man—half wolf, half demon, from one sniff. When red light shines from his hands onto Alaric's back, I'm certain he is a demon of some kind even when he looks pretty human-like. He has ash grey hair braided back, a full beard, and he has a sea-blue checkered shirt tucked into jeans. I don't know what he is, I've never seen a demon do magic like that other than Caspian, and it wasn't the same. This magic feels soft in its nature and I realise it's healing Alaric somehow. Half wolves, half demons are so rare and it's insane I've now met two of them that can use demon magic. Magic that is nearly gone from the world.

Alaric wears no clothes other than trousers, now soaked in the water, and I try to calm my heartbeat, my natural reaction to seeing his muscular chest and how spectacular he is. But there, hanging around his chest, is the mark of the alpha. A crystal, an enchanting deep sea blue stone, held in a circle of diamonds on a chain that makes a wave around the stone. It's the Rivermare symbol, his mark, and the stone is worn by every alpha for this pack. I remember the Caeli alpha's white stone and the Stormfire alpha's red one. All of them were said to have been given to their ancestors when they made their packs. A gift from the Mother herself. A blessing.

He's an alpha. Ancient, powerful, and devious enough to sneak into hell.

When he told me he had secrets, I never in a million years would have expected this.

"What should I call you then? Alaric or Lyulf or Alpha?"

My question hangs in the air between us as I feel like I can't suck enough oxygen back into my body. Having feelings for someone that has lied to you really sucks.

"Leave us, Denzel," Alaric commands.

Denzel looks tied between healing his alpha and listening to his commands, but he inclines his head, the red glow disappearing. Denzel walks down a stairwell in the ground and then there is silence—an uncomfortable silence—as we stare at each other.

"I'm sorry for lying to you about who I was," Alaric claims. "My middle name is Alaric, only my close friends know it, and I do prefer that name over Lyulf. Lyulf was my father's name."

"Why were you in the trials?" I coldly ask.

He leans back, wincing, and I hate myself for caring. For wanting him to call back Denzel to heal him. "For you. I was told of your existence and I felt your presence in my dreams, calling to me. You called to me or the Mother did. Either way, I was sent there."

My heart pounds in my chest. "Caspian, is he—"

"I got him out before coming for you," he tells me. "I'm not a fan of the half wolf, but I know you are."

Knee shattering relief makes my body feel weak for a second.

"At least he didn't lie to me about who he was and why he helped me. Did you know I was the first female alpha to be born?" I question. I need to know the truth and hear it from his lips, even if it will feel like a Band-Aid being pulled off.

"Yes," he says plainly. "And I swear on my life to never lie to you again. Never, Lilith. I vow on the Mother, on my pack, and on every bit of my soul."

Tears sting my eyes as I turn away from him, needing a moment. "I can't trust you anymore, Alaric."

"I understand." His voice is thick with emotion. "But I'm going to earn your trust back. What we have is too special, Lilith. I've waited what seems like a million lifetimes to meet you. To know you. To—"

"Enough," I cut him off and stand up, letting the water drip down my thick dress. "Forgiveness shouldn't be begged for. It can only be earnt in our world. I need to be away from you, Alaric, as I can't think with you here."

His eyes, once the colour of honey, are now crystal blue, brighter than the sea or the sky, and they search my eyes. "Okay. You've met my omega and healer, Denzel. He is downstairs and will show you to a room. I won't push anymore, Lilith, but we must talk."

"Am I safe here?"

"Yes," he firmly states. "No one will get to you in my pack. We are Rivermare, and we hold strong."

"No one knows much of your pack. You're known as being the only alpha in the world that doesn't trade or socialise," I say. "You keep sea monsters away from humans, but no one knows how you do that, and I know nothing that makes me calm about being here."

"Other than the fact you know, in your soul, I wouldn't hurt you," he counters. "And I saved your life, Cas' life, and got you out of hell. If I wanted you dead, I could have left, and I didn't. You might not know my real life, my title, and my pack, but you know my soul. And don't you dare say you don't."

"Alpha Lyulf, I wish to be alone," I coldly say, making my voice as impersonal as I can. His eyes narrow, and he stands, blood dripping from his shoulder into the crystal blue water around us as he walks up to me. He doesn't touch me, our bodies a breath apart, and he can no doubt hear my heart beating.

Not from fear or desire—from pain.

I trusted him, and I don't know if I can anymore.

Turns out my heart is more tender than I thought. I let him in too deep.

"You were terrified with Rizor, broken and bleeding on the floor in pain. I ran to you, breaking every law in our world to save your life. I put my pack on the line to save you, Lilith, do you understand that? I've risked hundreds of thousands of lives, and the sad thing is, I would do it again, even as you look at me like that. Like I've broken you," he breathes out. "I will do it all again as long as it ends with you safe. So hate me, Lil. Hate me as I watch you survive, thrive, and I will smile as I thank the Mother."

"Gods, please leave," I hoarsely whisper, tears freely falling down my cheeks as he steps back and climbs out of the water. He leaves me alone in a pool, my heart fractured and cracked.

I sit back down, letting my legs float in front of me as I try to calm myself. I don't want to leave this room while I'm still crying. I can't be seen as weak, not like Rizor thinks I am, because this pack will be watching me closely. I've put them all at risk.

I hear footsteps just before a woman appears at the top of the steps; the first thing I notice about her is her scent. She smells like spring, like the first floral breeze and it's intoxicatingly sweet.

I've never scented anyone like her, and I crouch as she comes closer, her long, white-as-snow hair falling around her shoulders. Her eyes are ever changing, like the ocean, swiftly moving between different shades of blue. In a breath, they are deep and dark blue like a storm, then they are the colour of the sky on a bright summer day like today. She's wearing a tight, dark blue corset, pushing up her large chest and a white skirt that falls to the floor with a long slit that reveals sharp daggers strapped to her thigh. On each of her arms are four dark blue, crystal bands with silver moons hanging off the top one on small chains. Her skin is dark, well-tanned and almost gold.

She crosses her arms, running her eyes over me in the same way I've accessed her.

"You're the female alpha, then. Honestly, you seem more badass in my visions," she claims.

I furrow my eyebrows. "Visions?"

"I'm fae. Yes, we do exist, and we see the future in the element from which we are born. Water, in my case," she says. "My name is Eulah of the Rivermare pack."

Fae? Fairies like my mother told me about in stories?

"Lilith...," I pause, unsure what pack to say I'm from now that I know the truth. Eulah seems to understand and walks up, offering me her white nailed hand. I pause for a second before taking her hand and climbing out of the pool of water, onto the cold stone. Eulah points to a pile of white towels, and I grab one, wrapping it around my shoulders.

"Come, I will escort you to your room," she instructs.

"I thought Alaric— Lyulf wanted Denzel to take me to a room," I say.

She looks back at me with her hauntingly mystic eyes. "Denzel is healing our alpha under my instruction. I don't bite... well, unless you ask, Lilith."

I clear my throat and follow her as she walks to the steps. Water drips from my body and dress as I head down the stairs, holding on to the towel on my shoulders that does little to dry me. The fae moves effortlessly, almost gliding across the floor, and my wolf is just as interested in what she is.

"I've never heard of fae existing in our world. Only that looking into the eyes of a fae could turn you to stone," I say, needing something to fill the silence other than my heartbeat and my wet feet touching the stone.

She looks back at me. The soft light from the hallway below us that is coming into view makes her look like a ghost for a second. "Earth fae do that. If I choose it, you could look into my eyes and I'd turn your body into ice. My enemies never stand a chance. Isn't it lucky I am on your side, Lilith?"

"Why, though?" I question.

"Because my loyalty is with Alaric. I was five when I washed up on his shore, thrown out of the fae lands by my parents."

"I'm sorry," I tell her.

"I was chucked into the sea because I was a bastard born. The sea gave me life instead of taking it because I was born in the ocean, and I see that as a blessing. Alaric nursed me to health and brought me up as his own. Though, now, we have a more brother and sister relationship."

I smile softly at her. "Your brother lied to me."

"He also went into an enemy's pack, risking his life for just the idea of you. You can't say you didn't feel the bond instantly when you met," she says, stepping into a corridor made from stone. The walls are pure grey slate, curved at the top, and there are several dark wood doors. The hallway is bright thanks to the wall lights, showing they have modern technology at least. Eulah leads me down the hallway to the fifth door and opens it, leaning her hand in and flicking on lights. "The Mother wanted you to meet, and you can't tell me her influence is ever wrong."

"I need time," I admit. "But thank you for your advice, Eulah."

She inclines her head, stepping back. "Use the phone and dial one if you need anything."

"Am I free to leave?" I ask her before she can walk away.

Eulah doesn't fully turn back to me but looks over her shoulder. "Soon, you will want nothing more than to come back here, to safety. You can leave if you want, but the world is looking for you. The world is a constant fight for power and you, Lilith, are the purest form of power that has ever appeared. The Mother sent you and many will want to claim you."

I shiver from the truth in her words, and I stay silent, watching as she walks away. I finally go into my room, shutting the door behind me and resting my head on the cold door for a moment before I burst into tears, letting the floor catch me as I fall. I don't know how long I cry on the floor, but by the time I feel better, I'm freezing cold and my wet dress is stuck to me. I stand up, peeling off my dress and wrapping myself with the damp towel before looking at my room. I pause, speechless at the view on the other side. There are four arched windows that are at least twenty feet tall, towering over the room, and each arch is shaped like a fish I don't know. I pass by the king-sized white frame bed with soft blue sheets and open the door in the middle of the archways, stepping out onto a balcony. This balcony is massive, wrapped around the room within the mountain. Part of the mountain covers half of the balcony, blocking me from view as I take in the sight. The Rivermare pack is in front of me, thousands of floating houses on top of a big lake. The whole pack is surrounded by five mountains. Each of the five mountains has been shaped, designed to look like sea monsters, and I can hear the sea nearby, waves crashing against rocks, mixed with the sound of the pack in front of me. The Rivermare pack is larger than I thought, or heard it was, and it's special. The balcony edge is made of blue metal, twisted to resemble crashing waves with fish inside. I feel out of place, my Stormfire blood so foreign to this regal pack ruled by Alaric.

The Viking wolf who tricked me.

We both tricked Rizor, and the thought makes me smile a little, knowing how pissed he must be. My smile fades when I remember Rizor and Eziel fighting each other and how Eziel might not be okay. I have to hope that Rizor wouldn't kill him because he is his son. Eziel, as strong as he is, is no fight for an alpha.

Gods, I'm an alpha. I don't have power, not yet, not without a pack, but it doesn't mean I can't make a pack somehow and gain that power, make it impossible for the world to ever call me weak again.

I wasn't born to be weak. I let the towel fall to my feet before I shift into my wolf, letting her take over as I rest my mind.

As a wolf, my heart doesn't ache so hard.

As a wolf, I can breathe.

CHAPTER 2

"Shift back," Eulah commands, looking over at me. I barely lift my head off the bed to look at her, my wolf having no interest in listening to a fae. In the corner of my eye, I see my bedsheets are covered in my red wolf fur and shredded to bits of fabric. I've really let her take too much control this time, in my need to escape my thoughts for a little while. My wolf huffs at her and turns away, only to hear her click her fingers, and the distinct smell of magic and water fills the room. I lift my head once more to see four spheres of water hovering above my head, threatening to drop.

The Stormfire side of my wolf isn't impressed, and she bares her teeth.

"I'll throw these at you for hours until you shift back. I want to talk to Lilith in human form," she commands, not fazed at all. "And don't you dare growl at me, wolf."

My wolf knows we don't have a choice, even if she isn't impressed. She lets me have control. We never refuse each other, it's the first law of being a shifter. We share a soul. Share. Even when my wolf is in a testy mood where fighting a fae seems fun to her. I force a shift back, red energy filling the room. I cover myself with the blanket after shifting back and smile tightly at her, brushing my messy hair away from my face.

"What do you want?" I ask.

"Are you always so nice in the mornings?" she questions with an arched eyebrow.

"Not to strangers," I reply.

"Ouch, that hurt," she says sarcastically. "This room smells like a wet dog, and your staying in here is pointless and only distracts my alpha."

"How will he survive?" I counter.

She shakes her head, annoyance burning in her eyes like a sea storm. "Get dressed, and I will wait right outside. Do not make me come back in here and drag your naked ass around the castle."

The water spheres disappear into a light rain that falls on me softly as she turns around and walks out of the room, shutting the door behind her with a bang. And she said I'm moody?

For a second, I wonder what would actually happen if I stayed in bed, shifted back, and completely ignored the world like I've been doing since I turned up at this pack yesterday. I've spent hours hearing people go past my doors or knocking on them several times. They always ask if I want food or something to drink. If I want anything. But I've said no to it all, just replying so they know I'm still alive in here. I've watched the amazing views of the sunset over the city, heard the sounds of nature and people echoing around me. I'm not sure what to make of it. This city is as big as Stormfire, but it's so different. It feels free, normal, and Stormfire always felt suffocating.

Alaric hasn't come, not that I blame him after how I left things. I'm not sure how to handle everything that's happened or how I'm feeling inside. Eulah is right. Staying in this room alone isn't doing me any good. It's not like I can sleep anyway, not with everything feeling lost. It's all still so raw, and I'm not sure I want to see the world and what is waiting for me. The pressure is now resting on my shoulders. I know Alaric is close by, feeling his presence as alpha and how strong he is. He is hundreds of years old, lived an entire life before we met, and I feel young and so stupid for not knowing who he was. It must have been so obvious to everybody else except for me. And we got close. So close that he stole a bit of my heart, and in the space left, there is only him.

I'm not sure I want that to leave. That feeling.

Reluctantly, I get myself dressed and brush the knots from my hair. I head outside my room in black leggings and a cropped night-blue top and sandals that are a tiny bit too big.

The clothes don't particularly go well with my hair or pale complexion, but it will do for now. Eulah is waiting with her hands behind her back, and she is wearing a strange sea green dress with four ropes tied around her waist.

"Don't dresses and long hair get in the way of any fighting you may need to do?" I question.

She smiles, and it's nothing short of feral. "I use my hair to strangle my victims and the dress to trip them up, not me. It's an art to use everything around you in defence."

"Plus, it makes you seem easy to beat," I reply, watching her bright eyes.

"Exactly. Wearing all leather suggests they need to be prepared. A dress lowers their defences, not mine. Males can be... easy to predict," she replies. "Come."

"Is Alaric easy to predict?"

"No," she says with a small laugh. "I see the future in the water, when I choose to, and his future is very unpredictable when it concerns you and this pack. The two of you are the greatest powers in his life."

"Me and the pack? Surely his people come first?"

"Before a mate?" she questions.

"I'm not his mate," I reply.

Her eyes sparkle. "I see the future. Do you want me to answer that truthfully?"

I pause, and she nods at me, seeing my unsaid answer. No. She walks away, no doubt expecting me to follow her at her side as we head down the corridors, all of them made of the same similar style, with rock walls and wooden floors. Eventually, they open up into a larger hall, which has four glass water fountains down the middle. Each of the water fountains are shaped like sea monsters, historic creatures curling up into the tall room with sharp teeth, the high ceilings holding them back from the outside world. They are so detailed that I wonder for a moment if they are real. The walls have lights on them, glowing softly, and several wolves are walking around, talking quietly. When I look back, I find dozens of eyes watching us.

"Don't worry, they're not just looking at you," Eulah says to me as we walk through and past the water fountains. "We are both a bit of a spectacle in this pack. You get used to it."

"Why do you live here? Not in your world," I question her. "I mean, I know you told me some things, but I'm just curious. Do you like living in the pack with none of your people here?"

"Yes," she answers. "My magic draws me back to the water once a month now to shift into my other form. A giant water and ice horse."

"Wow," I whisper. "You shift?"

"Yes, but only once a month. Any more and I'd never be able to shift back," she explains to me. "Wow, that's amazing," I say. "Fae are shifters of sorts, just different."

"You could say that. I am one with the water, but so are the rest of my kind, and they see me as a traitor, an outsider, and they try to kill me each month when I shift. For one day, twenty-four hours exactly, I am in the water where it's just me trying to survive against them all."

"I'm sorry they are so cruel," I tell her.

"Don't be sorry. I am lucky the Mother and the other gods chose to keep me alive and sent me on this path," she says to me as we walk through a large, ivy covered archway onto silver stone floors in front of a long descending row of stairs. There must be thousands of steps, and I feel my legs already groaning in annoyance before we start heading down them. Either side of the steps are rows of beautiful green, blue and yellow flowers on the hill in lovely formations, heading all the way down the street. We stay silent as I think over her words and take in the city we are approaching. There are about five rows of houses before the huts start on the lake, and many floating pathways in the middle of them. Children run past in groups, laughing as their parents chase after them.

I feel the happiness of this pack like a sweet embrace.

"Did Alaric send you here to get me out?"

"Quite the opposite. He told us not to leave you alone because that is what you want," she replies.

"I was wrong," I admit.

"I know," she says. "I've tried locking myself away, drinking my depression away and none of it worked. Accepting your life is a way of healing."

"You mean accepting this pack?"

"I will admit I want to convince you that we're not evil. This pack isn't so terrible," she tells me. "Come, I want to show you how wonderful our pack can truly be."

And so she does. For the next few hours, we walk around in the beautiful huts on the water, saying hello to several people that come up to us. We try beautiful and unique foods, stand in the sunlight watching it glitter against the water. I admire the glass sun-catchers hung outside of all the houses, casting such beautiful light everywhere. Eventually, we find ourselves sitting at the end of a piece of wood that hangs over the lake, watching swans and ducks swim about in total peace. The water floats around Eulah's feet softly, gently, droplets of water floating in the air around her like the water wants her back. That she isn't meant to belong here.

"Tell me what it's like in the fae worlds," I ask.

Eulah doesn't look my way as she speaks, watching the water like she can see the fae world in its depths. "I don't remember much of it, to be entirely honest with you, and what I do remember, I don't know if I've dreamed up. I was very young when Alaric found me, but what I do remember... I will share. It was beautiful, so beautiful that it hurt my eyes to look at it. The colours are unseen in this world, and they would burn the minds of humans to look upon the Fae world.

The air was so sweet that it was almost painful to breathe in, and the whole world itself was addictive and unusual. It made me never want to leave."

"There was no darkness, no evil, nothing bad ever around that could possibly make you doubt the beauty of the place."

"That's impossible. Everywhere has evil," I reply.

"Certainly not there, not in sight," she says. "The royal family kill anything that could possibly ruin their lives, their world, i.e. a bastard born, royal child like myself."

"You can't destroy the bad to save the good. There has to be a balance," I say. "And I'm so sorry they don't see that. Perfect isn't real."

"Perfect isn't achievable," Eulah agrees. "There are other, more powerful things to attain. Like love and family. Kindness and bravery."

"Do you ever want to go back?"

"No, my heart's not there, and it is with this pack as yours should be," she tells me. "I hate to tell you this, but there's no way that you'll be staying here long. The alphas of the world are not just backing down and letting Alaric have you. You'll be demanded to go back."

"I'd rather die than let Rizor have me," I answer. "He claimed to be my mate, but it was a lie. He rejected me, but I was never his to begin with."

"No, you weren't," she agrees. "This world is still ruled by men. Life is way too long for females to never have a leader. You are a blessing, Lilith. You are a blessing sent to us by the Mother, and for her, I'll fight for you."

"I would be honoured to have you at my side," I say.

"Show this world what a female alpha can do."

I intend to do just that.

CHAPTER 3

"You called for me?" I question as I walk into the large room guided by a man who shifted into a dark-blue-furred wolf the moment he told me Alpha Lyulf wanted to see me. I've given up trying to keep track of the long corridors, the archway shaped doors and the many, many empty rooms we have passed on the way here. This room is a level below mine, but I don't know much more. Alpha Alaric is sitting on a large leather chair in front of a dark wooden table with several leather chairs dotted around it. The table itself is one massive piece of wood, shaped into a leaping wolf, and Alaric is near the head of the wolf. His necklace catches the sunlight shining through the thin white curtains of the five archways that lead to a balcony, blowing in a lovely, sea-filled breeze. I can taste the salt in the air, and as much as I was used to snow or ash, sea salt is more refreshing. I brush my hands down the skinny jeans that feel like a layer of skin and resist the urge to mess with my halter-neck white top, which has a built-in bra.

Doesn't make it comfortable, but I look good at least. I've pulled my hair up into a high ponytail; the tips of my hair brush the middle of my back as Alaric inclines his head my way. The same tension that's always been there is still brewing in the room.

Alaric pulls out the seat next to him, clearly offering it to me, and I turn to see Eulah looking at me from the other side of the table. She's wearing similar clothes as yesterday, but this time all sea blue, and several silver necklaces fall to the middle of her chest. I walk over and take the seat next to her. She doesn't comment on it.

"Good morning, Lilith. How did you sleep?"

"Fine," I reply tightly because I hardly got any sleep at all. Alaric flashes me an amused and wicked grin.

We are all silent and I'm about to ask why I've been called here when two Rivermare wolves come into the room, shifting back into very naked men. I turn away as I hear the rustle of clothes and only when that stops do I look at the men. They are clearly related, their faces are so similar but pretty much everything else is not. One of them has light brown hair with blond tips, a cut on his cheek that looks old, and bright green eyes. He cautiously watches me, assessing me. The other one seems kinder. At least my instincts suggest he is. His hair is shaven, short, his eyes the colour of coal, and his lips tilt in a welcoming smile. Despite everything, I'm glad to meet other wolves and be out of my room after I spent my night in my bed wallowing, unsure what to do next, staring at the ceiling, wondering what Caspian's doing or what the prince is up to. If they are alive. If they are looking for me or thinking of me at all. The truth is, I miss them, and I'm not sure how to move forward until I see them. All my enemies that I seem to have acquired overnight are also a reason to escape that room, my thoughts, my anxiety over the future. Alaric wants to protect me... but how? How when the world is finding out what and who I am? My body feels restless as I sit here, moving slightly in my seat.

"Lilith, this pair, who are late, are my betas. Beta Beolagh and Beta Naithi," he introduces. "This is Lilith Thornblood."

I watch them both for a second, figuring them out the best I can before turning to Alaric. "Why am I here at this... meeting?"

Alaric picks up a glowing purple envelope, and it floats in the air in front of him, filling the room with the dark scent of demon magic. I glance at Alaric for a moment too long, watching the purple glow highlight his sharp features, high cheek-bones, and silky soft blond hair. Under this light, I can't imagine how I ever thought he was a normal wolf and not an alpha.

He radiates power as effortlessly as he looks handsome.

I pray to the Mother for my heart to stop beating so fast as I focus on the letter. It looks like it is wrapped in a hundred odd silver chains: the chains moving on their own, alive, reminding me of snakes. It is dark, dark magic.

"This came in the morning. It appeared when I was in bed," Alaric explains. "Set my whole bed on fire if you are inclined to know. Damn demon magic."

I tug my eyes up to meet his icy blue gaze. "Still doesn't explain why I'm here."

"It's addressed to us both," he tells me. "And you need to drop blood, willingly, on it to open. We both do."

"Interesting demon magic," I say, feeling more uncomfortable about this letter the longer I'm here. "Do you know who it's from?" I ask.

"Come here and we shall both find out, Lil," he gently suggests. The betas and Eulah are silent as I climb out of my seat and walk over to their alpha. Being near him is a special kind of torture for both my wolf and me. His scent wraps around me, lulling me closer, and it takes a lot to shake that kind of seduction off. I never realised it before, or truly accepted the pull, but it's always been there.

That's why, from the start, I trusted him. My wolf trusted him.

I guess it's why his betrayal has cut so deep.

Alaric slides out a dagger from under his blue cloak, and I offer him my hand. Softly taking my hand, he very carefully slices a cut in the middle of my palm.

I close my hand over the letter and let my blood drip onto the envelope where it sizzles. Alaric does the same, his blood slowly dropping. The second it hits the letter, it drops onto the table. The chains fall away until they are nothing more than silver littered about.

I look up at Alaric, and I nod at him. He picks up the letter, and I spot there's a seal on the back, which he breaks as he opens it, but I quickly recognize it as a Stormfire pack symbol. I've seen that horrid mark burned onto Eziel's back, and it's not something I could forget. Alaric is tense as he pulls out the long letter inside.

I lean over his shoulder as he reads it out loud.

Alpha Lyulf of Rivermare and Lilith of Caeli,
You have been formally summoned at dawn
tomorrow to The Pax.

If you refuse, it will be seen as an act of war.
Every pack on Earth will destroy Rivermare until
there is nothing but ash and fire.
She is not yours, and Lilith, you are not his to
claim.
Make your choices wisely.
Rizor, The Stormfire Alpha.

laric is silent as he slowly rips the letter up before growling as he throws it across the room.

"Lilith, do you know what the place you have been summoned to is?" Eulah asks me.

I shake my head at her. It's a familiar name, but I can't place where I've heard it.

"It's a place that was created in the Mother's image, and it's hallow ground. Absolutely no one can shed any blood or hurt anyone on that land without bringing about a terrible curse to themselves. No one's ever tried it, mind you. But no alpha, or supernatural, in their right mind would dare do anything while in The Pax lands."

"So it's safe?"

"As safe as a sheep walking into a herd of wolves," Alaric mutters. "Fuckkkk."

"As my alpha not so politely put it, it won't be safe, but to ignore the summons... well, it might not be in your best interest. From that summons, I'm gathering Rizor has told Caeli and Terraseeker's alphas about Lilith."

I hold my head high. "Then we go."

"No," Alaric growls, slamming his hand on the table. "I didn't save you from near death to give you back to him so he can kill you. He wants you dead, Lilith. Dead."

"He won't kill me there. Eziel's told me his father worships the Mother," I say, remembering that conversation in training because he rarely spoke of his father.

"I can create a portal exactly to the edge of The Pax lands. So you step straight into the lands, leaving no space for anyone to attack you," Eulah says. "I will reopen a portal when you call, Alaric."

Alaric looks sharply her way, his eyes glowing, his body tense and radiating alpha power. Enough to make it hard to breathe from the pressure in this room. Damn, he could bring the entire mountain down if he wanted to.

"I. Said. No." He grits out each word slowly.

"I don't mean to interrupt ya both," Beta Beolagh says, his thick Scottish accent making it difficult to understand. Damn, he is brave. "Alpha, is this female really worth the thousands that would die to protect her?"

Okay, not brave. Just stupid.

Alaric straightens up and very calmly walks around the table before he snaps. He grabs Beta Beolagh by the neck and slams him onto the table. I flinch at the cracking sound.

His brother, or however they are related, sits still like this is normal.

Alaric peels his lips back in a snarl. "Are you questioning me?"

"N-n-oo," Beta Beolagh manages to gasp out. Alaric looks up at me, sheer dominance and power shining in his eyes. "The answer to your question is yes."

My heart pounds as I take in what his words mean. He would go to war for me, fight all the packs in the world.

Mother above.

Alaric lets his beta go, snarling at him once before going back to his seat. I stand up. "No, I can't let you do that for me, even if I appreciate your protection, Alaric."

"This isn't up for—"

"It is, because this is my choice, and with or without you, I'm going to The Pax. I may have been born an alpha, which I'm sure is public knowledge by this point, but does it mean I will ever be an alpha to a pack? Will the Mother bless me? Who knows? Thousands and thousands of years ago, loads of alpha males were born, but it didn't mean they all became alphas of packs. A lot of them died, lots of them were hunted and some the Mother altogether ignored, and I could just be like one of them. Forgotten in the history of time. My only power is being an alpha female, the first one, but that title is it. Does it make me any better than any woman, child or man that walks the streets of this pack?"

I pause, letting my point sink in. "I will answer my own question, it doesn't. I will never let them die for me because I've done nothing worth dying for. I wouldn't and couldn't demand their life to be given up for mine."

There is silence in the room as I sit back down, Alaric's eyes burning a hole through the side of my head. I can feel his displeasure wrapping around me.

"As much as that's very noble of you, your life would not be forfeited that easily. I have no doubt that the alpha of Stormfire wanted you dead because you are a great risk for power. There's never been an alpha couple in the entire history of the world," Beta Naithi states. His accent isn't like his brother's, and it sounds familiar to me, perhaps Welsh, but I'm not entirely sure. It is just as near unrecognisable as the other beta.

He tensely smiles at me, cautiously picking at his words. "Could you imagine it? Two alphas ruling a pack, equal in power. Then the children you could have with an alpha, true born alpha children. That's never happened before. You could potentially have other female alphas as children and therefore make the world extremely powerful. You are a queen in a game of chess and everyone from the king to the knights will want you for power."

It's a thought I've had more than once, and every time I've thought about it, the more it scares me. I'd never have children in this world if they would be targeted from the second they breathed. They would never be safe, and frankly, I'm not now.

"I'm surprised Rizor wanted you dead at all. Surely, it's smarter to use you for breeding," Beta Beolagh points out.

"Don't talk about her like that. In fact, stop talking altogether before I drown you in your seat, wolf," Eulah warns, and Alaric shoots daggers his way.

"I would appreciate it if you didn't ever speak about me as if I'm a breeding machine. In fact, you should never speak about any woman that way," I say, defending myself. "May look sweet and innocent or whatever it is you see me as, but I'm not."

My wolf snarls in agreement, desperate to jump across this table and rip the beta's throat out. Thankfully, for the beta, I'm more rational than my inner wolf who has a slight problem with violence.

Beolagh inclines his head before looking up. "I apologise for my harsh words."

Something in his eyes makes me not quite believe him.

"So are we going, Alaric?" Eulah asks, getting us back to the point.

For a moment, I wonder if I out spoke and pissed him off. He is the alpha, the only one in the pack to set rules and boundaries, and I just told his beta off. I'm starting to have this zero give a shit policy now and I'm done not calling people out. I won't be spoken to like that.

Alaric slowly smiles, showing me he approves, and I straighten my back.

"We will go, Lilith," he agrees. "Prepare every-thing, Eulah."

"Of course," she says, placing her hand on my shoulder after getting up and leaving the room.

The betas bow their heads before following after her.

"Why is he your beta? He's a dickhead."

Alaric laughs. "Beta Beolagh is a prick but one of the most loyal wolves I know. He didn't make a good impression today but give him a chance. You'd be surprised."

"All right," I say, pushing my seat out. "Am I free to go back to my room?"

"You're free to do whatever you want in my pack," he tells me.

"I feel like a bird in a massive cage, unaware I'm not free because the space is too big to see the edges. But it's still a cage."

Alaric grits his teeth. "Is it really that bad here?"

"While I'm here, my brother is out there and could be used against me. Cas is out there, Eziel too. I'm worried. Your pack is beautiful, and if I came here before Stormfire, I'd never have left. But I can't just ignore the danger my loved ones might be in."

And that's the truth. Had things turned out differently, I could have been truly free here if only my mother came here with me as a baby over Caeli.

Something changes in his eyes, the anger melting away. "I have sent all my spies, hidden in each pack, messages about your brother and Cas. I've heard nothing."

"And Eziel? The prince?"

"Alive and well, as far as I've heard," he softly tells me, climbing out of his seat. "Come with me."

I climb out of my seat and follow him out of the room, down several corridors, glimpsing at the mountains outside the windows, the rising sun behind them making them glow. We pass through several massive state rooms, coming to a small spiral staircase. We go all the way down to the bottom, a few hundred steps that make my legs ache before coming to metal gates. I can instantly sense demon magic on them. The room smells of it, thick and dark and unnatural.

"How do you have demon magic down here? I thought it was rare?" I question.

"For the right price, nothing is rare in this world," he counters, and with his still bloody hand, he reaches out into nothing. A flash of red is all I see before the magic disappears from the room, leaving it silent. Small spotlights line the ceiling, making it bright in here, but it's freezing as Alaric pulls out a key from his pocket and unlocks the lock before letting me in. The small stone corridor leads to nothing for a while until opening up into a huge room full to the brim with weapons and objects, boxes, and crates. Many of the objects and weapons feel magical, but I'm not sure what sort of magic they hold. The ceiling is littered with jars filled with fluffy creatures floating inside of them that I've never seen before. They look alive as they look around the glass jars. My heart hurts for them. Nothing living should stay in a jar.

"You lock up living creatures?" I whisper.

"No," he replies. "Well, yes, but they are very dangerous pests that could not be safely released into the world. We catch them in the sea now and then when we calm the sea monsters, usually after they've killed a few hundred humans. Honestly, if I let all these out, they'd burn the pack down. And then the world. They're ancient, older than I can imagine or ever know."

"They look like balls of black fluff," I mutter, shocked.

"We call them Celtics and these were caught by my father and his father before him," he says, picking up one of the glass jars and bringing it to me. Inside it looks like little bundles of black fur and they spin around water really quick, smacking the glass occasionally. "I detest locking anything up," he agrees with me. "But when I took my father's pack, he was very firm on the promise to keep these things locked away unless I wanted to destroy the world. The worst part is they have bred over the years and there's more of them than there ever have been. I have nightmares about them escaping."

He shivers and carefully puts the jar back.

"So, the big, bad Alpha of Rivermare is scared of black balls of fluff?" I joke.

"Don't tell everyone. I have a reputation to keep up," he says with a deep laugh. I chuckle with him.

I clear my throat when I feel a little tension in the room. "So, did you bring me here to show me the fluff balls?"

"Actually," he says. "That's not why we came in here."

He leads me to the back of the room and opens up a large chest on the floor. It creaks as it opens, dust puffing out. It hasn't been opened in a long time. He lifts several pieces of paper up before showing me a very, very beautiful blue dagger resting on top of other weapons and tiny jewellery boxes.

The weapons glow with their own power, blue and dark, mixed with the odd red tendril of power. "These were my mother's," he gently tells me. "I promised my father I would not share this with anybody except for my mate."

"I'm not your mate, Alaric," I whisper.

He looks over at me. "If you're not destined to be my mate, then there will be no other. It's only you, Lilith. I knew it the second we met."

"Alaric," I whisper softly. "I wish you'd told me the truth."

He cocks his head at me. "At this point, me too, and for that I'm sorry."

"I know you are," I reply.

"I don't have a lot of my mother's things left. She died giving birth to me," he explains.

"I'm sorry," I say.

"Me too. I've heard that she was a fierce and beautiful woman. That if she picked up any weapon, it became magic itself and no one could stand in her way. Honestly, my people thought she could have been an alpha in another life," he says with a smile for his mother.

Losing my own mum, I know his pain. At least a little of it. I had time with my mum, and he has nothing other than stories.

"When my mother was pregnant with me, she boxed this crate and claimed it was for the alpha female her son would mate with," he says and goosebumps litter my skin. "That's what my aunt told me."

"Is your aunt still alive?"

"She is, and she'd very much like to meet you, but I don't know if you're quite ready for that," he replies with a smile. "She can be fiercely brutal with her words."

"Then I definitely want to meet her," I counter.

He chuckles low. "I'll invite her if we make it back from the Pax lands."

"Thank you."

"This box is yours with no catch," he firmly tells me, and when I open my mouth to say anything, he speaks. "If I'm blessed enough for you to be my mate one day, then I will be happy. If not, the box is still in the right hands. Take it. Please."

Hearing an alpha say please is powerful, and I feel like I'm looking into his soul, seeing the truth to his words as I answer. "Okay, I accept it. Thank you."

"There are other things besides weapons in here," he says, searching through the box. "But every object is magically enchanted by my mother. She had rare gifts. Fae blessed."

He lifts out a small book, handing it to me. My fingers brush his as I take the book and open the first page, seeing inside there are detailed drawings. Each page is littered with them and paragraphs with small descriptions underneath.

"My father gave each one of these weapons to my mother as anniversary presents to honour their mating over the years. Like a little tradition, I suppose," Alaric tells me. "This one was the last gift given before she died."

He pulls out a small leather box and opens it up to show a beautiful blue stone ring. My eyes flicker to the ring Eziel gave me, nestled on my hand, before going back to the ring in Alaric's hand.

"I'd like it if you'd wear this," he says. "This ring magically changes when you shift. It will turn into a band around your ankle, and it's also brilliant. No magic can be used on you while you wear it. It's the oldest ring in my pack, and my father never told me where it was from. My aunt doesn't know either."

"Are you sure you want me to wear it?" I ask.

"Yes. It will also stop any fae enchantments working on you, along with demon magic. I mean, the only fae I know living in the city is Eulah, and she would never harm you, but that doesn't mean the world's not full of creatures that are becoming aware of who you are and that puts you in danger."

"Why would the fae want me?" I ask.

"The fae have wanted a permanent place in this world for a long time and I imagine a female alpha as their bride would definitely give them that," he warns me. "You are power, Lilith Thornblood. Pure power, and I'm the only alpha who isn't going to try and take that from you. I want you to burn anyone in your path with it. Even if that means me."

He lifts my hand, and I let him slide the ring on my finger, the finger next to Eziel's ring. My skin burns from his touch, lighting up all of my body, reminding me of Japan. As I look into his eyes, my heart pounds as I remember the soft touch of his lips. How he felt pressed against me, his hands stroking my body alive.

"Thank you for this," I say, clearing my throat as I stand up. I'm too vulnerable around him, and I can't think straight. I need to focus on tomorrow and everything that is going to bring.

"I will get someone to bring this to your room," he says.

I nod. "Goodbye, Alaric. See you just before dawn tomorrow."

"I'll be waiting," he says, and I don't think he means just tomorrow. I leave him alone as I walk away, but I know darn well that part of my heart is always going to stay with him. I already gave it to him.

CHAPTER 4

The water portal appears like a giant spinning tornado, swirling and shaping itself into a wall of crystal-clear water. I tighten my hand into fists and meet Alaric's gaze. He's already looking down at me. In the water, our reflections shimmer, and the blue cloaks falling off both of our shoulders are a stark contrast to my red hair. We look powerful.

We look like alphas.

The strand of white is showing once more and my cerulean eyes mirror the colour of the water.

"Are you sure you're ready for this?" Alaric questions.

I nod. "I'm not a secret anymore, and I'm not pretending to be one either. I'm an alpha female, and I can't stand down. I can't hide," I say, turning my eyes back to the portal. "And I won't. This discussion is about my future, and I will attend."

"Very well said," Alaric comments. "And, might I mention, you look sexy as fuck when you're being commanding."

I chuckle and take a deep breath, glancing at E once as she holds the portal open. She nods as I walk with Alaric and into the water—which feels like cold air—before I smell the forest and open my eyes. Broken sticks and bark crunch under my feet as I feel the ancient, old magic of this forest sweep over me. In the centre of a forest full of large oak trees is a platform made of white stone and in each corner is a statue of a woman wearing a veil, holding up the roof with her bare hands. The statues are incredible, so tall and imposing.

The Mother watching over her forest, her sacred temple.

But this time, this place is filled with the dark, different energies of alphas.

My throat constricts as I set my eyes on Eziel sitting next to his father. I want to run to Eziel, thank him for trying to save me, but Rizor's eyes are pinned on us. Both of them wear dark red clothes, the Stormfire colours, and look regal in every sense. The Terraseeker alpha sits on his own, deep, earthy green clothes and a glowing emerald necklace encased in gold with a snake wrapped around the top. I meet his dark eyes before looking over, expecting to see my old alpha.

Instead, I find his son watching, and he isn't alone. Mathi—no Alpha Mathi, judging by the snow-white crystal necklace he is wearing—has a female here.

Not just any female.

My best friend, Aurelia. Her eyes find mine, and she tenses just a little bit before smiling softly. She looks thin but still beautiful beyond compare, and I'm glad to have her here. Even if it's at Mathi's side.

She had to pick the asshole alpha of the pair.

Alaric gently places his hand on the small of my back, snapping me out of the moment and guiding me into the temple. The stone table is the shape of an eye, and in the centre is a water fountain, which pours green water into the nooks, disappearing into the solid table. I can feel the magic in the air of this place and the water... it's something else.

We sit down opposite Eziel and Rizor in the two empty seats, the silence tense.

Alaric breaks it. "You called? Did you have to choose such a sacred place to discuss this?"

"You forget who stood here as each word was carved into the sacred stone in honor of our beloved Mother." Rizor's lips curl in a derisive smirk. "I suppose a lot of you were only pups back then." He pauses on Alaric in particular, and the two of them indulge in a silent standoff for a moment; their hatred for each other gleams in their eyes as vividly as the stars in the night sky. "How time flies when you're having fun."

A low growl rumbles in the depths of Alaric's throat. "Why did you bring us here?"

"It was not me," Rizor replies dryly, slouching onto the highest chair like a king holding court. "But I do believe the one responsible has just arrived."

There's a whoosh of hot air that sweeps around me, followed by the lingering scent of demon magic. It's familiar, dark and seductive, but it's not quite right. Something's off about it.

I turn to see Caspian and Leo arriving with another man between them. Caspian ignores everything as he storms over to me, immediately drawing my attention to him. I stand up just in time for him to embrace me. I breathe in his scent, feeling his heartbeat through my chest, and everything feels normal for a second. One beautiful, wonderful second.

"Let her go before I rip your head off, boy," Rizor growls.

Caspian ignores him and slowly breaks away from me. "You good?"

"Sorta," I reply, unsure how to answer anything else right now.

He searches my eyes, apparently finding what he wants, and he looks over my shoulder at Alaric. Whatever passes between them is silent and quick, but I saw something. I glance over at Leo, who looks between us both. Leo hasn't changed much since I last saw him. The same short haircut, his white hair still doesn't have an ounce of colour to it, and his eyes make my heart hurt in my chest. He's all the family I have left.

The demon seems amused, his bright eyes gleaming like amethyst stars. He's young looking, maybe only a few years older than my brother and Caspian. He has a navy waistcoat draped over a crisp white shirt, the sleeves rolled up to the elbow, and a pair of dark trousers clinging to his legs. A glowing red crystal on a silver chain hangs from his waistcoat pocket. The color matches the burning red of his hair that falls over his shoulders. His forehead is marked with red crystals, too, each one pressed into his skin to form the shape of a crown.

Everything about him screams seduction. From his muscular body and slender waist to his devilishly handsome face, it's difficult to look away. But Caspian is still more, in every sense, than this demon is or will probably ever be. Still, he's striking.

"Son, you never said the alpha female was beautiful as well as powerful. The Mother made her in her image it seems."

I tense at the demon's words. Wait. This is... Caspian's dad? Who's a demon Lord?

If that's the case, I must be wrong about his age. They look more like brothers.

Caspian looks straight at me. "The Mother made her more beautiful than even she could ever be."

"Brave words in her temple," the Terraseeker alpha warns, his green eyes shining.

The demon lord shrugs. "We are demons. The Mother already hates us." He trains his gaze on me. "Allow me to formally introduce myself. I am Lord Dyrk Hardling and it is an honour to meet you. I can taste your power and it does, indeed, outshine us all."

Despite the unease creeping into me, I nod respectfully. "I'm Lilith Thornblood. I'm sure Cas has told you all about me."

"Oddly, my wayward son does not speak of you much. But when he does, his eyes remind me of his mother and how she used to look at me."

"Father," Caspian growls at him, but Lord Dyrk just looks more amused.

So does Rizor, too, now that I look at him. No one else looks amused or happy by the demon lord's arrival, though. Not even Leo.

Leo watches me silently. "Can I have a private word with my brother?" I ask.

"No," Rizor snaps. "We don't have all the time in the world for you to chit chat."

"We don't need any time to converse, Sister," Leo coldly replies. I flinch from the blatant dismissal in his tone. "Lord Dyrk does not need to be here longer than necessary."

I glare at him, hoping to mask my hurt. "Fine."

Rizor groans and rubs his temple. "Gods, young wolves make my head hurt."

"Has all the innocent blood you've been drinking gone straight to that head of yours, Rizor?" Lord Dyrk crosses the length of the clearing in long, confident strides, his beautiful face wiped clean of emotion. "For if my eyes do not deceive me, I do believe you're in my seat."

Rizor's lips twitch. "Merely keeping it warm for you, *my lord.*"

Slowly he stands, just an inch or two taller than the demon, and stares down his nose at him.

The demon just smiles as if it's amusing to him. "Next time, don't."

Then he sits and shoos Rizor away with a flicked hand. I almost think Rizor's about to strike the demon, but then he moves to the last vacant chair.

The demon sits and clears his throat. "You all know why we're here.

"Each of us wants to claim the first female alpha in existence as our mate." His eyes flick over to me and linger for a moment before swiftly moving on. "Now, since only one of us can do that, the Crescent Mother has made it so that a series of trials will be held to test who amongst us is worthy of her gift. The alpha who proves himself by winning the trials will, therefore, win the female who, as I'm sure you'll all agree, is a prize unlike no other."

My stomach heaves, and I nearly vomit in disgust. Prize, gift, female. I'm just an object to them, something to be fought over and won. It's horrifying. Yet even my guys are listening intently, as if they're actually wanting to take part in this.

The demon lord stands and approaches a strange cauldron-like bowl made of sandstone. He waves a ringed hand over the empty surface and water quickly fills it.

He addresses the alphas then. "Those present who wish to enter the trials come forth." Now he withdraws a gold knife from his pocket and cuts his palm while Rizor and another male with bright green eyes follow suit. "You will vow to the Crescent Mother that should you ever spill the alpha she-wolf's blood, may your own blood be spent and your withered corpse remain." His blood drips into the cauldron. "I hereby make such a promise. I vow never to harm the prize in which I seek to prove myself worthy of claiming."

He's followed by Rizor and the green-eyed alpha. Alaric is next, and one by one, all the males make their vow to the goddess. Only Mathi is last, and it's because Aurelia is practically sobbing on his arm. Under all my rage bubbling away deep inside, a sharp pang of guilt stabs me.

I glance away, unable to watch him throw Aurelia off so he can pledge a vow I want no part in.

Once all those wishing to compete have made their vow, Lord Dyrk turns to me.

"Lilith Thornblood, as you are the prize in which the alphas must prove themselves worthy of, for each territory the trial takes place in you will be placed under the appropriate alpha's protection. This means you will be bound to them for a period of seven moons precisely."

I'm surprised steam doesn't come out of my ears when I finally find my voice and shriek, "*What?!*"

Everyone trains their eyes on me. I probably should have chosen a better word, but it's too late now.

"This whole thing is insane," I say, my chest rising with panic. "Vow or not, some of the alphas here would rather see me killed than protect me." Rizor smirks at me in a way that says I'm dead meat. I flick my chin at him. "He's not even hiding the fact that he wants me dead."

Rizor drapes an ankle over his knee and shrugs. "I'm afraid this is just my face, little mate.."

Son of a bitch.

My brother clears his throat, drawing the spotlight's attention to him. "My lord, do you really think this is wise? Perhaps my sister can stay with—"

The demon cocks his head just so in my brother's direction. "Are you questioning the will of our Mother, Leonidas?"

The blood drains from my brother's face, and he inclines his head in an act of instant submission. What the fuck is going on here? This demon lord has even got Leo wrapped around his finger. I never thought I'd see my brother whipped and under the thumb like this. The Leo I grew up with was always so confident—overconfident, actually —whereas this isn't the brother who proudly told me he was leaving home to become the best Demon Hunter in the world.

My heart sinks to my stomach. *What has Lord Dyrk done to you?*

"In which territory will the first trial be held?" I ask the demon, ensuring my voice holds more confidence than I actually feel deep down.

The demon gaze cuts briefly over my shoulder, then zones back in on me. "One I believe you are already familiar with." He pauses. "Stormfire."

My heart stops for a second. Of course it would be Rizor's territory. Not only am I being treated like an object to be won, but my first captor is the wolf who rejected me and killed my mother. Then tried to kill me. He might have taken a pledge to inflict no harm my way, but I highly suspect he's already thought of ways around it.

Leo must think so, too, for he steps forward to whisper in the demon's ear. Whatever he's saying clearly has a negative impact on the demon, who lifts a hand to silence my brother.

"Enough," he warns. "The Crescent Mother wishes the first trial to be held in the birthplace of the Demon Trials. As this falls within Rizor's territory, he will be the one to host Lilith during her stay there."

My brother nods and moves back. However, in contrast, Caspian glares at his father, and the two stare each other down for several tense moments.

Something glints in the older demon's eyes, and reluctantly, Caspian averts his gaze to the ground. I can tell by the vein pulsing at his temple how livid he is. A quick glance at Alaric and Eziel confirms that they're just as troubled by this as I am.

"How long will she be visiting each territory?" Eziel asks in a deep voice steeped in dangerous intent.

The demon glances at him. "Until the trial is over and an alpha has won. This allows for one week." He trains his gaze back on me. "I suggest you use this time to better acquaint yourself with your potential mates."

Suggestion fucking denied, I almost scoff at him. My brother's warning look silences me. As if delighted by Stormfire being the first territory to be visited, Rizor chuckles and latches his gaze with my own.

"Am I truly so mesmerising that words fail you, my sweet little Lilith?

I look the smug bastard dead in the eye. "Repulsive, more like. You *disgust* me!"

He laughs again, but there's no mirth in his eyes. No humour. He turns to face the others. "Now do you see, brothers, why we must prove ourselves worthy to claim this alpha as our mate? Her words are sharper than her bite. Believe me, I know."

My blood boils in my veins as I glare venomously at him. "You are many things, Rizor. A monster, liar—cold-blooded murderer. But worthy?" I scoff at that. "That's something you will never be. Perhaps you will learn that in the trials before you break your neck and die for good this time."

For a brief moment, Rizor's expression is unguarded. He lifts his brows and parts his lips slightly in what appears to be surprise. I can't help but smirk at his reaction. A few of the other males smirk, too, and none of them try to hide it.

Only the demon remains stoney-faced, apparently unamused by my hilarious sense of humour. He probably thinks I meant the joke this time, and he'd be right.

I *do* hope Rizor breaks his neck, and there's only one way to increase the chances of that happening. So before anyone can stop me, I withdraw the blade from the sheath on my thigh and clench it over the cauldron. Droplets of blood trickle through the gaps in my fingers, threatening to fall into the sacred water and mingle with the blood of the alphas. The instant realisation dawns on the others, there's a scuffle behind me and a hand seizes my arm. But I squeeze and let my blood dilute the water while clearly stating the oath.

"I, Lilith Thornblood, hereby enter *myself* into the Demon Trials. I will do as the goddess Herself once did and fight for my own freedom. For my own future. May the Mother bless me."

No sooner does the last word leave my lips when an uproar of protests explode from the infuriated males. Caspian's grip tightening on my arm draws me to him. He stares at me as if I've lost my mind. Maybe I have. But I refuse to let any of these males control my destiny.

"Do you know what the fuck you've just done, songbird?" he hisses in my ear.

I pull back and search his wide eyes, surprised by the anger I find burning there. I thought he'd be relieved because when I do win, I'll be able to choose my own mates.

Stay with him and the others.

"Of course I know," I say defensively. "I entered myself into the Demon Trials." Sweeping my gaze around the clearing, I catch the eye of each alpha wolf glaring at me. "And I'm going to win."

The Terraseeker alpha stands from his chair, his silver hair catching a ray of moonlight. "No, sweet pet, that is not what you just did." He smooths an elegant hand down the front of his clothes. "You disobeyed our Mother's wishes. Never before has such an act of defiance been done."

I lift my chin, more to conceal the tendril of unease that creeps over me. "Indeed. But then again, never before has there been a female alpha. Maybe it's time we shake traditions up a bit. If I had my way, I'd erase this ridiculous trial entirely."

More whispers, mostly in enraged disagreement, break out between them.

I wipe the blood off my dagger on my clothes and then sheathe it. Regardless of how I try to hold myself tall, that uneasy feeling continues to grow inside of me. The Terraseeker could be right. By entering the trials, I may have just placed myself on the Crescent Mother's shitlist. But I'm sure, from all I know of her, that she'd have done the same thing if a bunch of males were treating her like a trophy and threatened to take away her freedom.

I don't care what the demon says. This isn't something the goddess would agree to, and it's certainly not something I'd agree to without putting up a fight. And this is the only way I know how to fight.

I slide a quick glance at my guys; all but Alaric are frowning at me. The Rivermare has turned his back to me, and his arms are crossed. The vein throbbing on the side of his neck gives me little hope that he approves of my decision. I can't blame them for being angry. I am risking my life at the end of the day. But it's a sacrifice I'm willing to make if it results in absolute freedom.

Broken from my trance, the sound of Alpha Mathi slamming his fist on the armrests draws my focus to him.

"This is an outrage!" He glares at me with sheer and utter disdain, and Caspian pulls me to his chest as if to protect me. It doesn't stop Alpha Mathi from looking at me like he wants to tear me into pieces. "A prize competing for the place of victor is ludicrous. She must be extracted!"

Lord Dyrk shakes his head. "You know as well as I do that anyone who takes the pledge must be given a chance to compete."

"And should any harm be inflicted upon her—" another alpha says, one I don't recognise. The dark green cloak draped over his broad shoulders shroud him in shadows, even most of his face. "Is that not cause for the goddess to deem our vow broken?"

Alpha Mathi nods. "Precisely. Any blood drawn from her flesh will see the end to ours. She must be protected, not for her sake, but ours."

"Aww, shucks. I always knew you had a soft spot for me, alpha," I say with a sardonic smile. "Was pinning me against the wall and growling to try and dominate me really to get your dear dad to stand down?"

Alpha Mathi's eyes narrow into cutting slits. "Do not confuse yourself, halfbreed. Until now, my father merely tolerated you for your family's sake. Something my family has long lived to regret. My father stepped down because he does not want to shoulder the protection of the pack in the times you have brought upon us, Lilith."

Caspian's grip on me tightens, and in the corner of my eye, Alaric straightens as if he's about to lunge for Alpha Mathi. Fortunately, Eziel stays him with a hand on his shoulder, reminding Alaric of the rules: no blood spilled in violence.

Not here, anyway.

He sits back in his seat but grips the armrests until his knuckles blanch white. I nod my thanks to Eziel and then look back at Alpha Mathi. Despite my effort to suppress them, tears of surprise and rage threaten to glaze my eyes.

My family merely tolerated you.

Of course he did. I was a fool to think otherwise, and truthfully, I always knew I was tolerated because of my mother and the soft spot the alpha had for her. Alpha Mathi is another matter.

Here I thought, out of all the other alphas, save Alaric, Alpha Mathi might actually want to help me because I grew up with him. I watched his relationship build, or try to, with Aurelia. The reality is that he couldn't care less about me, and for whatever reason I can't seem to explain, the realisation stings deeper than the cut on my palm.

Why the hell do I even care about what he thinks about me?

I'm not in his pack anymore and I never will be again.

As soon as I win the trials, I'm going to create my own pack, and only three males present here will be welcome. Well, four, if I include my brother, but something tells me he'd rather be sniffing up his demon lord's ass.

Aurelia stands, walking to a corner of the room as the alphas continue to argue. I stand, leaving them to it and going to see if I can do anything for Aurelia.

"I'm so sorry," I gently tell her. "Mathi is—"

"Was mine," she growls, turning on me. I take a step back, shocked at her outburst. "I promised myself to him in front of my mother only two weeks ago and since he heard about you, it's like I don't exist! I'm nothing and once again, the unique, beautiful and special Lilith gets everything!"

"I get everything?" I angrily snap, well aware everyone must be watching. "Everything? Are you fucking kidding me? I lost my mum, was on the run, worked my ass off hiding in Stormfire and that ended up with me nearly being beaten to death! Now I'm being sold to the highest fucking bidder and you think I have everything? I'm sorry you chose a prick for a potential mate but don't you dare compare us. Don't you dare say I got what I wanted. I didn't ask for any of this, and I certainly don't want it. So fuck you."

I storm away from her and her shocked eyes to stand next to Alaric's chair, needing him close to me. He looks up at me, his eyes soft.

"On that sour note, I believe we are done for the day," the Terraseeker pack alpha claims.

Without thinking, I lean down and kiss Alaric's cheek. "I will be fine."

His eyes look up at me. "Be brave and know that I, like the sea, am always waiting."

My heart pounds in my chest, jumping and beating to his words as I know I won't ever forget them. Cas takes my hand and tugs me back into his arms.

"You're my best friend, songbird. I won't be far. I never will be."

A portal filled with crimson light appears behind Rizor. Digging his fingers callously into my arm, he tears me from Caspian's grasp and drags me toward the portal. My skin crawls at the contact, and I try to yank my arm free, but he just tightens his grip as he simultaneously uses his other hand to wave derisively at the others.

"May the best alpha win, brothers," he sneers, then he forces me up the stairs. "Let's get going. You and I have a lot of catching up to do, little mate."

And with that, he shoves me through the portal before I can even say goodbye to my guys. All I catch is their stunned, angry expressions before the light swallows me up.

CHAPTER 5

I stifle a yawn with the back of my hand, a futile effort to mask my exhaustion. But it's too late. Some of Rizor's wolves glance my way, and they grin as though their alpha forcing me to stand while everyone enjoys their feast is just entertainment for them. I suppose I am entertainment for them. Rizor wants me to suffer in any way he can that doesn't violate his pledge to the goddess. He's a cunning son of a bitch, I'll give him that.

The exhaustion tugging at my bones and the hunger gnawing at my stomach are beginning to make me delirious. And the wolves devouring their elaborate feast is torture.

My vision blurs, and I sway a little, unable to hold myself steady. I'm left with no choice but to balance myself against the side of Rizor's chair, which draws his attention to me. A malicious smile contorts the alpha's features as he sinks his fangs into a juicy chunk of meat. Blood trickles from the corners of his mouth, and in spite of my efforts, my mouth waters, causing my stomach to rumble with hunger.

"It appears our guest of honour is feeling tired," Rizor says, wiping his mouth with the back of his hand. His eyes gleam in the candlelight bleeding from the scones overhead. "Come, little mate." He stands and offers me a hand. "Allow me to escort you to a quiet place where you can rest."

Dark, sinister chuckles echo around me.

I straighten in spite of my exhaustion and keep my attention forward, refusing to accept the alpha's proffered hand. In doing so, he grabs my arm and drags me across the hall in swift, brutal heaves. The instant he touches me, sensation returns to my body, and I resist him, but any attempts to break free from his grasp result in sharp claws digging into my flesh. Even though I want nothing more than to claw at his smug face, there's a part of me, to my utter shame and disgust, that's thankful for the support.

I don't think I would've managed much longer standing there.

The doors to the hall slam behind us. Rizor storms down the granite staircase and enters a foyer where flaming arches and pillars twined with burning leaves decorate the floor. Rizor dismisses the guards with a wave of his hand, then he drags me under another flight of stairs, but this time there's a door. He yanks it open and drags me over the threshold.

Darkness envelops me until my senses acclimate. Meanwhile, I tear my hand free from Rizor's and wipe my palm down my front. He glances back at me with a chuckle and then opens another door. This time, a stone staircase leads down into even more darkness. But there's a light at the end, glowing softly, which weirdly helps control the tendril of unease creeping into me.

Rizor steps aside and bows low to me. "Ladies first."

I stare him dead in the face. "Then what are you waiting for?"

His smug grin fades as though melted by the fire he so clearly favours here. "I see you've still got that fire in you. Good." He opens the door wider and motions for me to pass through with a flick of his chin. "You're going to need it."

Despite the promise of cruelty in his face, I hold my head high and enter the stairwell. A cold chill sweeps over me. It's odd for me to ever feel the cold like this. My breath streams out before me as I descend the stairs one by one. Rizor echoes my footsteps. If it weren't for the vow he made to the Crescent Mother, I'd almost think he was about to kill me.

This is the perfect place to do that.

A swift kick to my back and I go tumbling down the stairs. A broken neck is far easier to explain than if he were to rip my heart out.

Cleaner too.

Fortunately, my vision has adjusted enough that I can at least see where I'm going, which is towards the light. But just to be on the safe side, I brace myself in case he does have any tricks hidden up his sleeves. He must sense my rising unease because he suddenly huffs a laugh under his breath. The monster is so close that his breath brushes the back of my neck, causing my skin to crawl.

"Fear not, little mate. I am not going to hurt you," he says at the foot of the stairs. "At least not in the way you might think."

My stomach churns, but I manage to school my features. "You're only saying that because you can't hurt me. You made a vow with the rest of the alphas."

"True, I did make a vow to not spill your blood." He digs his fingers into my shoulder and roughly forces me to turn left. "And I will honor that vow, pet, or may the Crescent Mother strike me down."

"Hmph. How reassuring. You so *very much* seem like a wolf of your word."

Despite my sarcastic reply, an insurmountable dread creeps over me like a shadowy veil. My breathing increases slightly, paving the way with small puffs of smoke. Then, with a final unceremonious push, Rizor shoves me toward the source of the light. The single lamp, dangling from the stone wall, barely hangs on by a thread, and it sways in the rainy breeze coming in through the mostly open ceiling.

That's not what grips my attention, though.

It's the dungeon in which the light bleeds over, reflecting off the silver bars. The only objects trapped inside are two dish bowls, the kind a dog would use and a blanket soaked in raindrops.

Home sweet home, I guess.

For now.

I know I shouldn't be surprised that Rizor would hold me prisoner while he can. However, as I take in the cruel environment I'll be spending the next week of my life in, I can't suppress the icy chill that sweeps over me.

Rizor approaches the gate and shoves an iron key into the rusted lock. He turns it slowly.

"The best thing about being the one who guards the Gates of Hell is that I've acquired a number of unique ways to inflict appropriate punishments." He turns the key slowly, his attention seemingly on the task at hand. But I know the sicko's actually enjoying himself trying to frighten me. "Sometimes the best way to break someone is by shattering the very thing they'd least expect to have taken from them."

I swallow my nerves and keep my head lifted high. "Oh, yeah? And what's that?"

He withdraws the key and opens the gate. "You're about to find out."

I clench my jaw and hold my head high, refusing to let him produce any fear in me. "Well, you do have a reputation to uphold," I spit derisively, entering the dungeon. I pause by the gate to look him dead in the eye. "Wouldn't want to disappoint fans of the almighty Inflictor of Pain, now would we?"

A cruel smirk upturns his lips. "I will be sure to never let that happen." He slams the gate over with a malicious wink. "Now, do make yourself at home. You're going to be spending a very long time here, little mate."

With that, he pivots and leaves me standing in the cold, wet dungeon. It's not until his retreating footsteps fade entirely do I release a breath I barely realised I've been holding. Or at least, if he does manage to, not give him the satisfaction of knowing he's achieved his goal.

I'd be lying if I said I wasn't worried about what his plans for me are. I know more than anyone how painful and erasable mental scars can be.

I wrap my arms around myself, both for comfort and for warmth, but the coldness in my veins still lingers. Droplets of rain trickling through the ceiling splash my head and draw my attention heavenward. Beyond the walls of my temporary confinement, the crescent moon gleams in the inky-black sky, giving me strength.

However, accompanying that wonderful strength is the reality of my situation. I'm alone and trapped in the Stormfire alpha's dungeon. I sink down to the ground, careful not to touch the silver bars, and close my eyes. Inwardly, I give myself permission to feel—to just process my situation. Yes, I'm cold and alone, but I won't be like this for long.

I have my guys to get back to, after all.

And if Rizor thinks he can break me by hurting them—he's in for one hell of a fucking awakening. And at least I do have one certainty in which Rizor doesn't. He can do whatever he wants to me because in the end, it won't really matter. By the time this is all over, Rizor will be the one to die.

Permanently this time.

* * *

"Psst, Redhead."

The quiet voice drags me from my cold, shivering nightmare.

Although, when I open my eyes and find myself curled up on the wet ground, my soaked clothes plastered to my body from the constant rain, it feels like I've been thrown into an even worse nightmare.

But that voice…

A panicked reaction grips me, and I search the dungeon frantically, praying to the goddess that Rizor hasn't captured who I think that voice belongs to.

"Up here," Knight says, drawing my attention to where the rain has finally stopped pouring through. The little demon peers through the window.

"Knight?" I whisper, wiping the water from my face to be sure it's him. I pale when I realise it is. "What are you doing here? Did Rizor bring you here? Are you hurt? What's going on?"

"These are all things"—he slips through the bars, dangling for a moment as he looks at me—"I am here to ask you."

He lets go before I can catch him. Fortunately, he lands on the ground safely with the lightest of thuds. He scrunches his little face in disgust when he scans the dungeon.

Despite every nerve in my body screaming for me to get him the hell out of here, my heart soars. After being in this hideous place for less than a day, it already means so much to me to see him. I have to remind myself that he isn't the most affectionate to keep from hugging him.

It's this reminder that makes me aware of the danger he's in. If Rizor or any of his mutts find Knight here, they'll torture him. He'd no doubt use the demon to break me. I can't even bear the thought, so I step back, away from him.

"You need to get out of here."

Knight cocks his head at me. "Why? I have only just arrived."

I shake my head profusely. "No. You need to leave quickly. It's too dangerous for you to be here."

The little demon just shrugs at me. "I may be small but I am mighty." He nods. "Yes. I shall stay right here where I am needed," he says, then he sits down crossed legged on the ground.

Although his concern for me is touching and brings a tear to my eye, I'd sooner sacrifice myself before letting any harm come to him.

I take a deep, shuddering breath. "Please go. I don't want them to hurt you, and they will if they find you here." When he makes no effort to move and simply crosses his arms in that stubborn way of his, I switch tactics. "Dragon needs you. He won't survive without you to keep him warm."

The gnome frowns at me. "What about Caspian? He can take care of Dragon. I will take care of you."

My heart squeezes in my chest. "Caspian probably needs you right now, too." I pause and bite my lip, recalling the state he was in when I last saw him. "How is he holding up?"

Knight draws in his bushy eyebrows and thinks for a moment.

"He's very lost without you," he says, gazing at the ground as though searching the empty space for something. "He has not left his room since coming home."

I frown at my hands resting on my lap. If Caspian is confining himself to his room all day, I doubt he'll take proper care of himself. He tends to forget to eat when he gets distracted. Or angry. From the last time I saw him, he's definitely the latter. I don't blame him. I'd be losing my mind, too, if he were taken away from me and I couldn't help him.

Knight's solemn expression hardens my resolve. I hate to guilt anyone into doing things they don't want to, but I will not have Knight imprisoned here with me.

Even if that means guilt-tripping him.

"Don't you see? This is why you need to go back. Dragon *and* Caspian need you." My statement draws the demon's focus back to me. "Don't worry about me. I'll be out of here soon." I glance around the dungeon and a tinge of uncertainty creeps over me. "Rizor can't keep me here forever."

Knight blows a raspberry at the mention of Rizor, then he says, "The half demon wishes me to give you this."

My pulse spikes as I watch Knight reach into his pocket. What would Caspian have possibly wanted to give me? Hopefully a way out of this place. Although I know the chances of that are slim, and even then, I wouldn't do it. Escaping here might compromise my position in the trials, and I refuse to let Rizor take that from me. Knight pulls out a folded piece of paper and hands me it. I immediately recognise Caspian's handwriting and my heart skips a beat.

I'm getting you out of here, songbird. Hang in there.

Tears sting my eyes and distort my vision as I hold the letter to my chest. Catching Knight's quiet assessment of me, I give a sheepish laugh.

"Men. Apparently all it takes to receive a love letter from them is imprisonment."

Knight nods. "The half demon's letter has made you happy."

"Yeah, it… it has." I inhale sharply and tuck the letter into my pocket, clearing my throat. "He can be a bit of a softy when he wants to be."

"Softy…" Knight frowns as if pondering the meaning of the word. "Not soft like the furbabies you speak of." His small hand touches my leg, the closest thing he ever comes to giving hugs, or showing affection for that matter. "Love. Because you are his family."

I smile at that. "Don't look so sad. I'll win the trials and be back before you know it."

"*Sad*?!" The demon shouts and puffs his chest out defensively. "I am not *sad*—I am *enraged*! A knight's job is to listen and protect his family, but you insult my honor by forbidding me!"

His angry rise in tone attracts nearby attention. An orange light appears at the top of the passageway and slowly bleeds a path down the stairs, each flicker accompanied by footfalls.

I grab Knight's hand. "You have listened to me, and you can protect me by going home." I lift him up despite his wriggling and protests. He climbs through the bars, his small legs struggling at first, then looks down at me. My voice breaks when I add, "Please, just get out of here. Go!"

Heavy boots echo down the staircase and the light draws closer. Knight stares at me long and hard for a moment before hopping onto the window. He's gone by the time a male figure stands in front of the dungeon. Weirdly, I barely felt the cold when Knight was here. Now I'm shivering again and the rain spitting through the ceiling lands on my skin like droplets of ice.

The male sneers at me as he slides a tray of food through a slot in the gate. From the force of his kick, the tray skates across the wet floor, and the bread rolls onto the ground, landing in a puddle.

"So very kind of you," I snarl at him. "Thank you for that."

"You're welcome... *alpha*."

He spits the word out and then makes his way back up the stairs. I glare at his retreating figure. As soon as he turns the corner, I hurry and collect the roll. But it's already like a sponge now, having soaked up so much water in such a quick time.

My stomach growls in hunger, so I bring the bread to my lips and eat it. Bits of dirt float in the plastic cup of water. I'm so thirsty that I don't care about that either. Beggars can't be choosers, and right now, I need to eat whatever they give me to keep my strength. How else am I to win my freedom?

As I drink the last of the water, I think about what the first trial could be. However, footsteps echoing down the stairs again pull my attention to the gate.

"What now? Time for my dessert?"

I expect the guard to appear, but instead it's Eziel. My heart soars with relief at the sight of him. It takes everything in me not to run to him. Tears blur my vision as he withdraws a metal key from his back pocket and opens the gate.

"T-two visitors in one night," I stutter from the cold, "I'm a l-lucky gi—"

He lifts a finger to his lips, signalling for me to keep quiet, and deftly twists the lock. I bite my lips to keep from speaking and watch him dip into my cozy little room. He barely steps inside when he shifts into his wolf and curls around me, resting his giant head on my lap. His body heat immediately transfers to me as I tenderly stroke him, savoring his warmth, his scent, his very presence.

Even in the darkness, my prince is here to keep me safe and warm.

A tear escapes my lashes despite my efforts to restrain them. It drops onto his temple, causing him to raise his head and lick my right cheek. I press my forehead to his and let my tears fall silently.

I've missed you, Ez.

CHAPTER 6

*S*leep is an escape from the cold, from the endless hours of pure silence other than the constant sound of water dripping down above me. But with endless nightmares of the past, nothing is a real escape. The small prison is still there when I open my eyes, my head flat on the ground, the dirt cutting into my cheek. I lift myself up, my bones aching from that small movement alone, and scan the dungeon. Eziel is nowhere to be seen.

Did I just dream about him last night?

Or did Rizor put some kind of illusion on me as a form of torture?

He wants to weaken and break me so that when his trial starts, I will have no hope of winning. My wolf howls for release in my mind, but I don't have the strength to shift into her. I can only tell it's been three days or nights, as Eziel always comes in his wolf form, staying close to me and warding off the sheer cold. I didn't know any place in Stormfire was cold.

The alpha who likes to torture has, of course, found a place to leave me where the chance of freezing to death is very likely. I rub my arm where I've lain down, feeling several sore spots from the uneven, rocky floor. A familiar lump swells in my throat but I swallow it down.

I will *not* break.

The door creaks open outside my prison and I force myself to stand and not show weakness. Soft fire light warms the cracks of the damp hallway as Eziel slowly appears. This time, he's not in his wolf form.

"Hi," I lamely whisper, but he doesn't smile, his eyes and body leaking with tension as he unlocks the door and comes to me. He wraps his arms around me, kissing my forehead as I breathe in his scent to comfort myself. Goddess knows how I smell. Not good, I imagine. "What are you doing down here?"

"Rizor sent me to escort you to be washed and dressed for a celebratory meal. Fuck, I hate him." He growls and cups my face, tilting my head up. "But this week is his only power over you, and then you can leave this goddamn pack. I will make sure he doesn't win this trial. The only person who should win is you."

I lean up, running my finger over a nasty scar on the side of his cheek. I've never seen that before. My stomach clenches.

"Was this Rizor?"

He nods. "I couldn't kill him. Fuck, I don't know why I couldn't."

"Because he might be a bastard, but he is your father and your alpha. Honestly, it would have been bad if you did kill him in anger. This pack is on tenterhooks and——"

"I'm not a born alpha," he readily answers through gritted teeth. "I'm strong, but I wasn't born an alpha."

"I understand, and it's why it will be me that ends his life. I am owed his life, and I can take the pack."

If I want to is another matter.

He locks his eyes with mine. "You won't ever be alone, Lilith."

"Does it feel odd to call me by my real name?"

"Not particularly. I always knew who you were," he states with a grin, and I mirror it.

"Is that why you decided to train me?"

He shrugs. "Nah. You just had a pretty ass that I wanted to stare at while you climbed the frames."

I whack his arm playfully. "Liar," I say with a laugh.

As if a light's been snuffed out, his humor vanishes, and he sobers. "Come on." He wraps an arm around my waist and leads me out of my prison. "The shadows are always watching and whispering to their alpha."

In other words, we need to be careful what we say. While I'm glad to leave, there's a part that dreads what fresh hell Rizor has planned for me.

We come to the door and climb the few steps to the top, pushing it open. The cold of the prison disappears, replaced with the warm heat of the Stormfire pack. I shiver at the feeling as I'm led through smooth gold corridors until we come to a room with two red wolves sitting outside. They part for us as we go through the doors to a bedroom that, guessing by the scent, belongs to Eziel.

"Is this your room?" I whisper.

"When I choose to stay here, yes," he replies and looks down at me. "I can't stay in here with you, but a friend of mine is coming to help you into the dress. Whatever you see tonight, remember you only have to be here until the trial, then it's over."

"Unless he wins," I counter, "and then this will be my life forever."

Eziel's gaze darkens. "He won't win," he swears. "I want to stay, but he is calling for me. Letting me come here, out of wolf form, is his way of reminding me who's in control."

I remember what it's like to have an alpha call for you. It's physically painful the longer you ignore the call and the fact Eziel is still here at all is a testament to his strength.

"Will you be at the meal tonight?" I ask before he leaves.

He shakes his head. "I have a feeling I won't be invited."

"Then go," I whisper, holding my head high, "and don't worry about me. I can do this."

His eyes burn with unspoken anger as he turns around and storms out, slamming the door at the end behind him.

I still feel frozen to the spot in the warm room until the door opens and a dark-skinned woman comes in, her bright blue eyes glancing at me as she shuts the door. She looks badass in all leather, her hair braided down to her shoulders and red paint marks running in lines across her high cheekbones. She's very thin, but her arms are muscular, and I bet she's stronger than she looks.

Her wolf is Stormfire, she smells of ash from the tree.

"Lilith Thornblood?" she asks in a curt voice, and I nod. "Don't tell me you can't speak."

"I can speak," I respond, surprised at her bluntness. "What's your name?"

"I was born to serve the alpha, and he has demanded I tell you my name is Fire as I have none. He calls all the royal slaves Fire as a reminder of what will happen to us if we do anything wrong," she replies. "It seems you have pissed him off."

Bastard. Everyone deserves a name.

I smirk at her. "He wanted me dead, and now I'm alive and he is forbidden to hurt me. What do you think?"

She sweetly laughs, shaking her head as she walks across the room and pulls back a sliding wooden door to reveal a bathroom. Fire turns the bathwater on, pouring in a purple liquid and stepping back. "I presume you can bathe yourself?"

"Yes," I answer.

"Good," she replies. "I will wait outside the door after getting your dress. Knock when you're ready."

"Thank you... Fire," I reluctantly say.

She smiles, leaning closer as she passes me, her voice nothing more than a whisper. "Make him pay, alpha girl. The city, the world, is singing your name in hope. Lilith Thornblood, the first born female alpha."

I will. I hope my eyes tell her that. I hope she knows I'm not giving up my power.

After letting the bathtub fill up, I strip out of my dirty clothes and climb in, wincing as the hot water smooths the cuts, scrapes, and sores littering my body. I didn't know how easy I had it in Rivermare, and I miss Alaric. I run his mother's ring around my finger, watching how the soapy water makes it sparkle.

I duck my head under the water, and I feel it. Something magical grabs hold of my senses and pulls my eyes open. Right above my stomach there is magic in the water, glowing like silver fish swimming about. But it's silver traces of power, swirling and creating a shape. It slowly forms a pair of eyes, then a nose, and finally a face shape.

Alaric.

He stares at me, the vibration of the magic shaking the water as we look at each other and just seeing him makes my heart feel warm. He mouths words to me.

"Are you okay?"

"Yes," I mouth back.

"I'm always here," he promises before whatever magic he used to see me is gone and I break free of the water, gasping for air.

"Goodness hell, girl!" Fire exclaims, her arms under my shoulders as she pulls me from the water like I weigh nothing. I cough and gasp on water as I climb out and she wraps a towel around me. "Were you trying to drown yourself?"

"No," I cough out. "It was... I fell asleep."

"You fell... asleep?" she asks, blatantly not believing me, and she shakes her head. "Let's just get you dressed, shall we?"

I nod and let her guide me back to the bedroom. She blow-dries my hair and draws wings of eyeliner on my eyes, and paints my lips red before showing me the red dress laid out for me. It's basically nothing and my gut turns at anyone seeing me in that. Fire doesn't comment as she helps me into the dress, which ties around my neck, covering my breasts with two thin strips of fabric and leaving a massive slit in the middle of them that reaches my stomach. The silk fabric is tight around my waist and four thicker strips of the silk fabric fall off it around my legs, barely covering my core. After sliding on red, shiny heels, I look in the mirror.

Mother above, I barely look like myself. I look like a slutty princess and if I were going on a date with the right wolf, I wouldn't care. But when I look like this for Rizor's pleasure, I want to be sick. I have to force myself to remember he can't hurt me, but he can embarrass me, and I'm sure that's what tonight is going to be about.

Fire bows her head when I turn to her. "Thank you."

"He is waiting, Lilith Thornblood," she says, not lifting her head, and I glance behind her, seeing the deep shadows of the room moving on their own. Watching.

I hold my head high as I walk out of the room, not that surprised to find Rizor waiting outside in the corridor, two wolves on either side of him, their red fur making them look like they are on fire. Rizor himself is bare chested, except for his necklace that rests in the middle of his chest. He has dark trousers and shiny shoes on and his arms are marked with painted fire in symbols I don't know.

He sweeps his eyes up and down my body. "You clean up good. At least the Mother made you beautiful, if not powerful."

"What could you possibly know about true power, Rizor?" I question. "Every inch of power you have has been taken instead of earned. There isn't a wolf in this pack of yours that would save your life if they had another choice."

He takes three steps forward, towering over me. "Like you? Alpha female Lilith Thornblood... of no pack. The Mother gave you power, but you have nothing. You're a prize in a contest for alphas, and if I win, you're dead."

My heart pounds even when I already knew this. "Rizor, it's almost sweet you think you can win this. You won't, of course, but it's sweet that you delude yourself into thinking otherwise."

He grits his teeth and turns away from me, his hands clenched. I know, if he could, he would be beating me right this second. I still remember every punch of his fists and kick of his boots like it just happened yesterday, but I refuse to show him fear. I refuse to let him see how much he can scare me.

"Come." He instructs, storming down the corridor. I walk after him, the two wolves flanking me. My heels clicking on the stone keeps my mind busy, focusing on the noise until I hear music. Mozart, I think, is being played on a loud piano and a woman's melodic voice singing a song about fire and wolves over the top of it. Wolf howls and growls drift to me along with their scents, the overwhelming smell of ash filling the room. I tense up before the clapping begins as Rizor walks into the room ahead, through large black painted wooden doors. I gulp as I walk in, unsure what I was going to see, but I scent them first.

Demons. Humans... wolves. Their blood is easy to pick up in the room, along with the scents of desire and sex. It all mingles, and I see why when I stop in the doorway. Humans and demons are standing on pillars, naked and bleeding as they hold different positions.

Living statues.

One human man catches my eye from a pillar and the emptiness in his gaze makes me shake in disgust, unable to hide my reaction.

The music carries on and the humans, the demons, move like dancers to it. Under the statues, I make out withering bodies pressed against each other, their moans and groans echoing. I look away, feeling sick at the sight. The wolf shifters, all in suits and perfectly shiny dresses, move aside for Rizor, and we follow behind, so many hushed whispers filling my ears. So many eyes on me, judging and wondering. I feel their happiness, their joy at all the suffering, and I want to scream at them, scream as I demand to know what the hell is wrong with their cruel and sick minds. My mouth is dry as we finally get to a long stretched table empty of people. Rizor sits down in the middle seat, larger than the rest, and pulls out the chair next to him.

I reluctantly sit down and tuck myself in, looking at the silverware in front of me.

"If you disapproved anymore you'd have it written on your head, Lilith," Rizor comments before clicking his fingers. "You ought to be a little more open minded, or you'll never survive in this world."

"This is *your* world," I snap in a whisper, "not mine or one I will ever be part of."

Rizor scoffs as two demons rush over, their skin bright green and without any hair. I don't know what kind of demons they are, but they make plates of delicious looking food appear in front of us with a wave of their hands before stepping back. The steam coming off the food only makes me feel sick. I haven't eaten anything but stale bread and drops of water off the floor in days, but I still won't touch this food while so many are suffering around me.

"Eat," Rizor instructs, tucking into his food.

"No," I respond.

He slowly puts his fork down and turns on me. I flinch, expecting him to attack me, but I soon remember he can't. "Many in this world starve as you refuse that food. It is rude."

I chuckle low. "Rude? Seriously, that's ironic."

I hear him gritting his teeth as I keep my gaze on the woman in a bright yellow dress, dancing on her own with several men looking her way. She is a good dancer. "Do you know my story of how I became an alpha?"

"No," I respond again.

He leans back. "I was born to a poor family of wolves, in no pack, and out of my five siblings I was the only one to survive. My father liked to beat us and my mother was long lost in her own world of denial and burying children. My father could never figure out what was wrong with me, as he had never met an alpha. There was only one, the Terraseeker alpha, around at that point, and it was too far to travel to join that pack. When I turned eight, I challenged my father's wolf in an argument, and he submitted to me."

I stay silent, unable to feel sorry for him because he has turned into a bigger monster than his father was. So many have suffered under his rule. "The next day he paid a demon to drag me to hell and leave me there to die. I remember falling into hell, down steps and waking up with this in my hand."

He lifts the necklace. "A demon lord found me, taught me and built me as who I am today before

I claimed my place as Alpha of Stormfire. You met him."

"Then you killed hundreds of demon lords for being more powerful than you."

He smiles like that is a fond memory. "I killed them because I *knew* them. I knew what they wanted, and trust me, the world is better off without their kind."

"What about Lord Dyrk?"

"He was the demon lord who brought me up, and he is an exception," he smoothly replies before changing the subject. "I never wanted children, did you know that?"

"You made that clear when you burnt your mark on your only son's back like he is an animal!" I snap. "Did you love your own father for being cruel? Did he inspire you to be so brutal to your own son?!"

"Shut up," he growls at me, slamming his hand on the table. "I marked my son because he was in danger. He isn't a born alpha and from the second he drew breath, every wolf and demon wanting power has tried to kill him. I marked him to save his life. It did save his goddamn life!"

Heavily breathing, we stare at each other. I still hate his guts, but perhaps he isn't the monster I painted him as in every sense. He is a monster with a story.

But he still deserves to die for what he has done, and I will always hate him. He killed my mother, forced me to be on the run, and destroyed my life. He rejected me as his mate for sensing a weakness he didn't like. I spent so much time wondering what it was he sensed, and I think I know now. He sensed that I loved my mother, that I'd die to save her. That I could love.

And love is a weakness to him because he never had it. He doesn't know what it means. I pick up the knife in my hand and flip it around before slamming it at his chest. He grabs the knife, cutting into his hand to stop me. I push down; the room goes dead silent as I push with all my strength. He grits his teeth, his blood dropping down between us as we glare at each other.

"Shame the Mother has my loyalty and I can't rip you to shreds, but don't for a second think you have enough strength to do this. To kill me," he says, laughing. "So many predicted your birth, sang songs and prayed for you. And here you are, weak. Powerless. The Mother hasn't even blessed you with a stone because she knows you aren't an alpha. You are nothing."

I scream as hands wrap around my waist, pulling me away as I try to fight them. Rizor's laugh is the last thing I hear before something hard smacks me on the head and I pass out.

CHAPTER 7

I rub the lump on the back of my head, a painful reminder of last night's events. This is *not* how I wanted to start the trials. While getting knocked out as a parting gift shouldn't have come as a surprise, I can't help but wince at the pain splitting through my skull like a hacksaw.

And the culprit's standing right next to me.

Rizor catches me massaging my head and slides me a cruel, derisive grin. *Fucker.* One day I'm going to get him back for everything he's done, and the rest of his pack better watch themselves the moment that I do.

Especially the one who did their alpha's bidding and knocked me out.

They're all going to pay for what they've done.

I glare at Rizor as he steps out of line from the rest of us and approaches his pack gathered around the *Tree of Ignis*. The ever-burning leaves flutter around him, but as always, they disintegrate into nothing more than ash. A warm breeze lifts them into the air and forms a silhouette that briefly shrouds Rizor in a veil of shadows lifting on the wind. His black cloak, threaded with intricate crimson patterns to represent his pack, billows lightly around his heels. I pray to the goddess that he meets his demise by tripping on it during the trial.

The Stormfire alpha, Inflictor of Pain, killed by his own ridiculous cloak.

How deserving a way that would be for him to die. If you're truly watching this, Crescent Mother, please grant me that one wish…

The whole 'death by cloak' thing is actually what prevented me from wearing the cloak delivered to me this morning by a Stormfire servant. Whatever Rizor has in store for us won't be easy, and I don't want anything to hinder my movements. Or Alaric's, which is why I convinced him to leave his. It didn't feel right for me to wear anything specific as I'm not representing a pack.

I'm representing myself and the things I'm fighting for: freedom and a little bit of revenge.

"So here we are," Rizor calls out for everyone to hear, "at the precipice of an event that will change the course of history for all eternity."

His wolves erupt into applause while I scoff and roll my eyes, briefly drawing Rizor's attention. I narrow my eyes into slits, but he just smirks at me. *Asshole.* Alaric laughs at my reaction and nudges my shoulder lightly with his. Okay, so maybe I'm here for more than just a 'little' bit of revenge. I'm here to win and watch Rizor suffer and wallow in his defeat.

Then I'm going to kill him.

While he continues on about this trial being a gift from the goddess Herself, I scan the crowd. As if drawn to him like a magnet, my gaze lands on Eziel at the front of the crowd. Caspian stands beside him and they're the only people who couldn't look more reluctant to be here even if they tried. For some reason, it makes me smile, that and the fact that they both look unharmed. Yet it's in seeing them that I'm reminded of how desperately I want to be with them again.

Soon, I remind myself. *You just need to win first.*

Caspian locks eyes with me while Eziel glares at his father droning on about how amazing their pack is. By the prince's look alone, he wholeheartedly disagrees. I scan Caspian's face and body. He looks to be okay. A little tired, and the marks on his face are glowing slightly which is not usually a good sign, but he doesn't appear to be suffering. Just extremely pissed off.

"I'll be okay," I silently mouth to him.

The muscles in his jaw tick, but he nods all the same, belying his faith in me.

I'm pulled away from him and back to Rizor at the mention of the trial.

A smile threatens my lips, but it dies when I hear Rizor's next sentence.

"The objective is simple," he says, motioning to the screen hovering above him. "Whoever captures the target will be awarded the point."

"All right," Alaric grumbles under his breath. "Let's see what this dick's got in store for us."

I follow his line of sight to the screen hovering nearest us, and my heart drops to the pit of my stomach. Our so-called target is no bigger than Dragon was when I rescued him. I've never seen this species of demon before. At least, I think it's a demon. It's more fox-like than anything and has one large flowing tail made entirely of fire. The tufts of fur poking out from its pointed ears are also ablaze, as well as its gold eyes, and its tiny paws are barely kitten-size.

"The winner will present the creature at tonight's feast," Rizor continues, "and they will also be the first one to eat it."

"Did he just say ea…" The blood drains from my face, and bile claws its way up my throat, cutting off my words.

Alaric gives a disgusted grunt. "Aye, he did just say that."

"But why? It's just an innocent little demon."

"It *is* very innocent," Alaric whispers, "and powerful, which is why Rizor wants one of us to kill it. He knows it'll upset you more than the rest of us. Might even convince you to pull out. Not to mention, Firespirits are notoriously difficult to locate, but if anyone knows their way around Hell I'm betting it's him. Wouldn't be surprised if he ends up cheating to spite us all."

My anger rises the longer I stare at the screens. Of course Rizor would plan something so cruel and barbaric. It's in his nature. It's as inherent to him as breathing.

The bile in my throat threatens to purge from my mouth when I let out angrily, "Just when I thought Rizor couldn't get any more disgusting, he does this. It's barbaric! I hope the Crescent Mother strikes him down—strikes you all down for wanting to take part in this."

"This is just the nature of the game, halfbreed." Mathi fills the gap beside me, snow-white cloak fanning the ground around him. "If you've not got the balls for it, the portal's right there behind you. Don't let it hit you on the way out." He smirks and then looks up at the screen. His expression sobers a little and a genuine look of curiosity claims his normally smug features. "I've never seen a Firespirit before. I read about them at the academy. They're one of the rarest demons in the world and are filled with ancient magic. The only way to get that magic for ourselves is to—"

"Slaughter it?" Alaric growls and clenches his hand into a fist, the effort straining his leather gloves.

"—sacrifice it to the gods and then eat its heart to gain its power," he answers with not a flicker of emotion. "Apparently it tastes like overcooked chicken. Or so the last Caeli who recorded it stated. That was over a thousand years ago, and a Firespirit has never been recorded since."

My stomach heaves, and I struggle not to rein in my own emotions. This is even more horrific than I thought. Why would the goddess even allow this? I steal a glance at the rest of the alphas, but none of them are even remotely fazed by our objective.

They'll do anything to win.

Even Alaric, as disgusted as he appears by the situation, carries a look of determination on his face that rivals the others. Is winning to them truly worth killing an innocent, ancient demon that hasn't been seen for over a thousand years? I frown at my boots cushioned by a thin layer of ash on the ground. The real question is if killing any innocent creature is worth gaining my freedom. Would I even be able to live with myself?

The crowd erupts into cheer. I look up just as Rizor briefly lifts his arms in the air and then saunters over to the base of the tree. Placing a ringed hand against an invisible lock etched into the side of the portal, the sapphire light turns crimson, mirroring the flaming leaves around it. Each of the alphas start making their way toward the tree, and I cast a final glance at Caspian and Eziel. Both of them look as grim as each other and sudden unease grips me.

"Whatever happens in this portal," Alaric whispers, taking my hand in his, "don't let go."

He brushes his lips over my knuckles, then slides his fingers through mine. His tenderness eases my anxiety somewhat, and I smile faintly. However, the screen displaying the adorable demon kills it.

"Rizor said we only need to catch the demon to win," I point out, my voice similarly low as we pause outside the portal, my hand still linked with his. "We're going to do this together, Viking, and we're gonna save this little Firespirit."

A broad smile lights up his features like a ray of sunlight. "Something tells me you plan on adopting it, too, like you did with those other furless babies."

I return the smile despite my rising trepidation. "It's furbabies, and hey, don't tempt me."

Alaric chuckles and with that we enter the portal together. In a few minutes, Caspian, Eziel, and the other competitors will follow. I just hope one of us finds the Firespirit before anyone else does.

CHAPTER 8

The air is ripped from my lungs the instant I step into the portal. I open my mouth to scream but nothing comes out, and my hand slips from Alaric's. The ground beneath me vanishes, and I'm falling through a bright white light in a downward spiral that seems to go on for eternity.

But then the light gives way to darkness and thick, sharp objects snag my clothes as I continue to fall. I blindly reach out to grab one of them. A sudden impact slams into my stomach as I'm thrown aside, into an even deeper darkness that penetrates and consumes my every sense.

What the hell is going on?

Another strange object hits me, this time on the back of my head—right where I was struck last night. *Shit!* My breath returns to me again, and I let out an enraged scream.

I will *not* die before I've even had a chance to fight!

Grabbing the dagger Alaric gave me, I stab blindly until I latch on to something. It's hard and smells like wood, but it doesn't hold me for long. A deafening shriek shrills around me and I'm falling again, only this time I tighten my grip so that I cut through the wood in the hopes it will help break my fall.

It doesn't.

Air replaces the wood merely seconds later, and I slam into the ground, the wind once again knocked violently out of me. Pain sears through my body, and for several moments I all but lie still, gasping for breath while simultaneously taking in my surroundings.

Despite the burning sensation in my lungs when I breathe, I'm able to take a deep inhale before I roll onto my back. The burning leaves smell is my first clue. The enormous roots scaling the walls and ceiling are my second.

I'm inside the *Tree of Ignis*.

Literally inside, cocooned by its giant, interconnecting roots that forge a tunnel around me. Every single one of them is filled with a softly glowing fire that pulses, reminding me of the veins coursing blood through my own body.

It's beautiful.

Ignoring my sore muscles, I rise to my feet and straighten so I can get a better look. My head nearly touches the ceiling. I duck, gently but cautiously pressing the back of my hand to the root above. It's hot but not scalding. Not like the root oozing a thick, golden liquid on my left.

Then it hits me that I'm to blame for this.

It was me who stabbed the *Tree of Ignis* and made it bleed.

I defiled something sacred and ancient, a creation which is precious to the Crescent Mother. The thought sinks my heart to the pit of my stomach. Closing my eyes, I rest my forehead against the root.

"I'm sorry I hurt you," I whisper, placing my palm beside my head. A solitary tear escapes my lashes and rolls down my cheek. "I promise to fix this."

Whispers echoing down the tunnel draw my attention back to the task at hand.

I step back and cast one final look at the root smothered in molten blood.

"As soon as I've saved the Firespirit, I'll come back and…"

I trail off as my teardrop seeps into the wood and a burst of sapphire light spreads up the root, healing it. It's as equally amazing as it is terrifying.

How the hell did that happen?

Unfortunately, the male voices shouting close by prevent me from finding an answer. Footsteps thump across the ceiling and the voices slowly begin to fade. I should follow them, see where they're headed. Maybe they've got a lead as to where the Firespirit is.

Returning my dagger to the sheath on my thigh, I check that my other knives are still intact and good to go, then I make my way quietly down the tunnel. I cast a final glance at the magically healed root before I disappear around the bend. There's got to be a reason my tears did that.

I step out of the tunnel and emerge into another. The voices have faded entirely by the time I reach the end of this one. But the roots are thicker and wider here, so I don't have to duck anymore, which is a relief. I'm also relieved that the fire burning within them is bright enough to pave the way for me.

"You sneaky motherfucker!"

A familiar and welcome voice stops me. "Alaric, is that you?"

There's a pause and then a lot of cursing. "Unfortunately."

"Where are you?" I search the tunnel again, but he's nowhere to be seen. "Are you with Cas or Ez?"

"Erm…" Another pause, followed by a deep, frustrated sigh. "Kind of. We fell down a hole."

My guys… are stuck in a hole? I bite my lip to keep from laughing. *No, don't laugh. This is a very serious situation.*

"How the hell did you fall into a hole?" I ask.

Alaric huffs. "You can ask Caspian that, if I haven't already killed him by the time I get out of here."

Still struggling not to laugh, I tiptoe forward in search of a hole in the floor. When I find it, I wince at the depth. It's at least a thirty foot drop.

I hope none of them broke anything.

I peer into the hole cautiously. "While I have many questions about all this, how do I get you out?"

"You don't," Alaric says. "You just keep going."

Caspian's voice echoes through one of the walls. "And remember that this place is a fucking maze!"

Alaric nods. "A living one, so be careful up there. If you fall through any of the traps—they appear out of nowhere—you'll need to work your way back up."

"It's a little like the game *Snakes and Ladders,*" Eziel, also somewhere nearby, chimes in.

Alaric winks at me. "Aye, but there's only one snake down here, lads, and he's not too happy about our girl being all the way up there." His grin fades as quickly as it appeared. He lowers his voice and becomes serious again. "You need to find the heart of the tree. That's where I think the Firespirit is."

I nod, grateful for the lead. "How do I find the heart?"

"The thicker the roots on the ground, the closer you're getting. That's all I know."

"Also, watch out for any damn puddles," Caspian shouts. "They're traps that appear out of nowhere and suck you in."

A look of genuine concern drifts over Alaric's face. "I know you'll be careful, and we won't be too far behind you, but if something bad happens—"

"Nothing bad will happen," Eziel is quick to argue. "If anything, the tree should be worried about what Lilith might do to it."

"Exactly," I agree, more to lessen their worry over my safety than anything. "I'll have you know I am very well capable of looking after myself. Most of the time." I stand, brushing the dirt from my clothes, and wink down at him. "First one to reach the heart wins. Loser cleans up Dragon's poops for a month."

He smiles and his piercing blue eyes gleam with mirth. "Get your marigolds ready, love. It's on."

Caspian chuckles from wherever he is. "Now that's the spirit. So get a move on, songbird."

I smile and continue onward through the tunnel. However, my expression sobers once I know he can no longer see me. I know the guys want to compete in the trials to keep me safe, and if I fail to win, to be the one who claims me. But I still care deeply about them.

"Lilith?" Caspian's voice catches me before I disappear around the corner. He sounds closer. "May the sexiest wolf win."

My laugh escapes me before I can suppress it with a hand.

Yeah, they're going to be totally fine on their own.

I turn the corner and scan the floor in search of more thick roots. These are disappointingly thinner than the ones in the tunnel I landed in, which means I'm going in the wrong direction.

Grumbling, I head back the way I came, much to my guys' amusement.

"Back so soon?" Alaric quips.

"Still stuck in a hole?" I shoot back, grinning at him. "At this rate, all three of you will be cleaning up after Dragon for the next four weeks. Don't worry. You can take turns with my marigolds."

Their laughter follows me down into the next tunnel, and I smile again.

Two additional tunnels later, I climb a set of stairs carved out of enormous branches twined together. I pull myself into yet again another tunnel and immediately scan the ground.

To my utter relief, the roots are at least two times thicker than the ones before.

Although there's been no signs of traps, Alaric did say they appear out of nowhere, so I lighten my footsteps and double check each placement just to be on the safe side. The fact that the roots are getting thicker means I'm on the right track, which is encouraging.

It also makes sense why the Firespirit chose to hide here.

The *Tree of Ignis* doesn't just possess the hottest flames of Hell. It circulates those flames to every other realm in the world. This is why it's always burning.

At the end of the next tunnel, I find another staircase. If I landed in the bowels of the tree, then to reach the heart, I need to keep climbing. I grab the branches for support and pull myself up. Thicker branches, wider tunnel, and a deep, steady thudding echoes in the near distance.

The heart. It's got to be the heart.

My own pulse spikes in excitement as I hurry towards it.

Until the beating noise is punctuated by a low growl that's way too close for comfort. I freeze to the spot and glance to the side, where a red wolf snarls behind me. It's not Rizor or a Stormfire wolf I recognise, but it's definitely from that pack.

Rizor probably sent it to kill me.

It snaps its jaw when I make no attempt to back down, and I curl my lips in a derisive smirk.

"Aww, you want me to let you pass? You'll need to catch me first, little puppy."

I might not be as fast as my four-legged enemy, but I'm a damn better climber in my human form, so I use it to my advantage. I break into a run and search the next tunnel. There's no stairs so I move onto the next one. At the same time, more paws hit the ground running.

Two wolves are hunting me now. How fun.

My heart leaps at the sight of the stairs and I run for them. Roots creak underneath me as a hole in the ground appears. I jump over it, just managing to avoid falling through. That must've been the trap Alaric warned me about.

I glance back in time to witness one of the wolves falling through it with an echoing yelp.

"Ooh, poor wittle baby," I laugh over my shoulder.

The tree's heartbeat is so close I nearly confuse it with my own.

I'm almost there!

But then, when I'm within reach of the stairs, a hole in the ground opens, and just like that I'm falling through a trap. Seconds later, I crash into the tunnel below. I land on my front and my breath is momentarily seized from the impact.

I shouldn't have laughed at the wolf. Karma can be a real bitch sometimes.

Wolf howls overhead drag me to my feet. However, my stomach clenches when I see the thin roots stretching underneath me. More horrifying than that is the Stormfire wolf lunging towards me. Time to get up close and personal.

I pull out my largest knife and prepare to fight. But it just runs past me without so much as a passing snarl. Confused, I spin around to frown at the wolf's retreating figure.

Then I see what the wolf is chasing.

At first, I almost miss it: the fiery ball of fur darting around the corner followed by even more red wolves.

They've found the Firespirit.

Before I even fully know what I'm doing, I shift into my wolf and chase after them. I will not let them hurt her; there's no need for it. I find the wolves cornering her against the stairs, where even more wolves snarl down the top of them.

Blinding gold eyes cut over the wolves' heads and land on me. It's not until a wolf growls from behind me do I realise she was trying to warn me. The wolf goes for my hind leg. I twist my body and sink my fangs into its neck, biting through until bones shatter under the pressure. The wolf's dying yelp attracts the attention of its pack mates.

I growl in warning for them to back off. The two wolves at the bottom of the stairs turn on me. At the same time, I lunge for them, and our bodies collide in the air. Claws rip into flesh, teeth crunch through bones, and blood sprays out, painting my vision with crimson rage and sweet promises of death.

A loud shriek escapes me as sharp canines embed in the side of my throat.

They clamp down and drag me to the ground.

I try to kick them off, but I'm soon pinned underneath a huge, powerful wolf, and it's not the one sinking its teeth into me like I'm a rare juicy steak. It's a different wolf, Rizor's beta, going by his sheer strength, and he claws at my face.

Darkness seeps into my eyes, and then light— bright, blinding, beautiful light—explodes around me as though I've died and the goddess Herself is carrying me to her temple on the moon.

My fiery hair floats around me as I drift in a sea of stars towards the most beautiful moon in existence. Its pale silver glow spreads through my body like a pleasant memory from my childhood. It's familiar and comforting.

It's Mother... and she's calling me home.

A happiness unlike anything I've known washes over me.

I'm coming home!

I reach out as if to pull myself closer, but something burns my hand and the moon shrinks. The stars dim, fading into darkness.

Panic and despair flares through me. "No, please—please don't go!"

I grasp frantically at the air and manage to capture a star. It bursts in my hand like a soap bubble, then each of the others start to pop, one by one vanishing into nothingness. The moon grows smaller while I fall into the void of nothing below.

I wake up with a gasp, but instead of stars I'm surrounded by fire and an echoing heartbeat that does not belong to me. Instincts immediately kick in, and I reach for my dagger, preparing to fight more of these Stormfire wolves even if it kills me this time.

However, I pause when I take in my injuries.

They're completely gone.

Only patches of dried blood remain where they should've been.

Someone must have brought me here to heal me. Alaric, maybe?

Still clutching my weapon, I search my environment for signs of him or any threats. But I'm seemingly alone inside what appears to be a cavern inside the *Tree of Ignis*. A huge waterfall made of fire plunges through the roots on the ceiling and into a pool of lava that streams throughout the cavern. I follow the trail to an enormous beating heart cocooned in a shield of roots for protection.

"I found it… the *Heart of Ignis*."

In my amazement, I all but forget that I might be in danger, and slowly walk towards the heart as though I'm dreaming.

It's just so beautiful. So... otherworldly.

Through the gaps in the roots, I'm able to see what the heart looks like.

It's shaped almost like a diamond—a monstrous, living and breathing diamond that breathes fire into each of the roots.

The scorching heat blasting off the heart threatens to burn my eyes the longer I look, but I can't seem to pull myself away.

So beautiful...

Rocks scuttling somewhere behind shocks me from my reverie.

I raise my weapon and pivot, expecting either Alaric—which would be an awkward greeting—or one of the other alphas. Or even more Storm-fire wolves come back to finish their job. But a tiny Firesprite stares up at me with unblinking gold eyes. It looks exactly as it did on the screen back at the Inner City, except for a blue crescent moon that glows on the middle of the demon's temple.

I sheath my weapon and slowly crouch to her level. "Now this isn't fair. How can something so cute be so damn lethal?"

The Firesprite tilts her head at me and one fluffy, flaming ear flops over the other. My heart just about melts in my chest.

"You have such an adorable, boopable little nose, do you know that?"

She looks down at her nose and wiggles it as if she understands what I'm saying. Or possibly offended by the idea of me booping an ancient Firespirit on the nose.

"I hope you're not offended by the whole booping thing." I smile and scoot over cautiously. "It's just my awkward way of showing affection."

She scoots over too and gently paws my leg; she doesn't burn me. It takes a moment for me to realise what she's doing. She's gesturing to where the Stormfire wolf sunk its teeth into me. Raising her other paw, she points to the dried blood on my forearm. I absently touch it while her message slowly dawns on me.

"It was you. You saved my life, didn't you?"

The Firespirit dips her head in answer.

A few minutes ago, my heart threatened to melt. Now it's bursting.

No, breaking, as the reason why I'm here dawns on me.

She's in danger.

"You need to hide. The others are still looking for you, and only goddess knows how close they are now." I jump to my feet and pace the area with nervous strides. "There's got to be somewhere you can go. Somewhere the alphas won't be able to reach. What about here? Can they get inside or is there a magical shield or…"

I trail off as the Firesprite trots over to the pool of fire. She sits beside the farthest away edge, glances briefly over her shoulder at me, then turns back to the pool.

Clearly she wants to show me something.

I approach cautiously and kneel beside her. She keeps her gaze rooted on the fire streaming back into the *Heart of Ignis*. Bubbles appear on the surface and create a strange rippling effect that forges images out of the magma. It's a symbol, one I vaguely recognise. I learned about this at the academy…

What was it again? Elemental something. Elementis? Elementai?

Elementum!

I read a story once about the Elementum guardians and how they're believed to be the source of all magic. They protect the realms and it's their souls that create the ley lines. Without them, we'd have no portals, no magic, nothing.

I turn to her in amazement. "You're an Elementum! Oh my gosh, of course. That's it! *Firespirit*. You're a protector of this realm. But… that doesn't make much sense. Why are you on your own?"

She looks over at the heart and whines. There was a section about the Elementums that claimed they could only become guardians if their path crossed with another soul they deemed equally as worthy.

"You've not met anyone worthy yet, have you? I suppose it's because they're too busy hunting you. Those assholes." I sigh and stare down at the symbol hovering above the fire. "I'll help you find someone worthy so you can be with the rest of the spirits. But first, we need to get you somewhere safe."

I press my hands into the earth and move to stand. The Firespirit lets out a high-pitched bark and paws my hand repeatedly. The crescent moon on her head glows a shade brighter when she touches my skin, and the *Heart of Ignis* thumps louder.

The Firespirit has chosen... me?

"Is it because I fought the wolves for you?" I ask, scarcely able to believe what's happening.

She nods and paws me again.

"Whoa. Here I thought I'd try sneaking you home with me once all this was over."

She huffs through her nose as if laughing.

"I guess you already are home," I whisper, looking back at the heart beating within the roots. Helping her become a guardian might be the best

145

way to protect her from the others, even if that means she'll disappear forever. "All right, Firespirit. What do you need me to do?"

To my surprise, she crawls onto my lap and tucks her bushy tail around herself like a blanket. I reach out and gently stroke her soft, surprisingly non-lethal fur, and the warmth radiating from her travels up my arm, spreading through me like sunbeams.

As I sit here stroking her, I hum quietly. It's a song my mum used to sing when Leo and I were kids. The Firespirit must like the sound of my humming because she nestles into me and her breathing starts to quieten. She must be getting ready to let go. I fight back my tears as best as I can and continue holding and petting her, but soon my sniffling gives me away. She glances up at me, and I give her a wobbly smile.

"I'm okay. Go on, little fox." I lightly tap her nose, whispering brokenly, "The spirits are waiting for you."

She smiles, genuinely smiles, before laying her head back down and then taking her last breath.

On the exhale, her eyes close tightly, and I know that she's gone.

A quiver catches my lower lip. I don't bother trying to stop it now that she's moved on. She needs to know how important her existence is in our world and how even a stranger will mourn for the brave sacrifice she gives.

I lean down to kiss the top of her head. "Thank you... for everything."

Her warmth slowly fades from my body and back into her own.

It's then her spirit appears in a small collision of tiny sapphire stars that huddle together. They drift over to the roots protecting the heart and then slowly merge inside of it. For a moment, the heart stops beating and turns sapphire, just like the stars. Then it thuds again and it's louder than before now that the Firespirit is finally where she's longed to be.

Home.

A portal appears behind me, pulling my attention away from her. The trial's over. I should be relieved, but I'm only angry. Angry that Rizor wanted us to kill—not only an innocent creature —but an ancient guardian of the realms. His cruelty knows no bounds.

This is just another thing he'll pay for once this is all over.

It's not until Alaric appears, slightly out of breath and flushed in the face, do I set her on the ground.

He glances down at her limp body and asks quietly, "Too late?"

"No. Not too late." I wipe the tears from my eyes with the back of my hand. "Just in time."

Alaric holds out a hand and helps me to my feet. "You won the trial."

"She wasn't just a Firespirit," I say, my voice a little shaky. "She was an Elementum."

His eyes widen in recognition, though he doesn't say anything.

"She chose me, Alaric, after I saved her from Stormfire wolves… after she saved me."

He squeezes my arm comfortingly. "Let's go. We can bury her by the tree."

I nod and he moves to lift her, but she turns into ashes.

Alaric scratches his head. "Well… here is also good too. It was her home for the past millennia, after all." He bends to cover her ashes.

"Wait. I've got an idea." Reaching into my pocket, I pull out two velvet pouches and sweep her ashes into them. "All right. Let's go. I'm sure Rizor is starving by now."

I tuck one of the pouches into my pocket, hold the other, and follow Alaric into the portal. The other alphas are just arriving when we reappear at the base of the tree. Out of all the people staring at me, I see only Rizor and the look of murder seething on his countenance. He watches me approach him through narrowed eyes; a predator who's been defeated by their prey.

This is a wonderful moment, one I commit to my memory forever.

I don't even hide my smirk when I stop in front of him. "You said the winner must present the Firespirit at tonight's feast. Well, since I will not be attending for obvious reasons… here." I slam the pouch into his hard, rigid chest. "Don't eat it all at once now," I add with a smirk.

He clenches the pouch with one hand and seizes my throat with the other while Alaric lunges for him.

"Rizor, release her," Lord Dyrk commands. "All have witnessed Lilith's triumph during this trial, just as all have witnessed your beta's treason."

A shackled male is dragged to the front of the crowd by two familiar faces.

Eziel and Caspian.

Rizor scoffs and faces the demon lord. "Koran and his men were not under my orders. They acted freely. Irrationally, but freely."

"Indeed, Father," Eziel agrees, "but their actions were still carried out *for* you, regardless."

Lord Dyrk nods and addresses the rest of the pack. "Koran and those who accompanied us will be punished for their treason. Lilith Thornblood will be excused from the feast while this goes underway."

I give the demon a grateful smile. "Thank you, Lord Dyrk."

He inclines his head and then saunters off, saying without a backward glance, "Come, Rizor."

With everyone still watching, he reluctantly releases me.

He brings his lips to my ear with a snarl. "You may have won this trial, little mate, but you better pray you lose the next. Or it won't be your life on the line."

Before I can throw back a spiteful retort, Alaric stands between us.

"You got that right. It'll be *your* life if you *ever* threaten my mate again."

"Rizor," Lord Dyrk bellows.

Alaric smiles and shoos a hand derisively. "Off you go now, back to your master."

After a long, strained moment, Rizor follows in the demon's wake. The wolves who tried to kill me are dragged off after them.

"Making friends everywhere you go, eh, halfbreed?"

I groan at the sound of Mathi's voice. "Do me a favour, *Alpha Mathi…* go fuck yourself. Preferably sideways with a stick."

Surprisingly, he just laughs before stalking away.

Alaric watches his retreat through hooded eyes. "The vow I made said nothing about hurting the Caeli alpha. Just putting that out there."

For the first time in a while, I laugh. "Right now, I'd settle for some alcohol."

Alaric bows and offers me his hand with a grin. "Your wish is ever my command, my lady."

CHAPTER 9

"Can we talk?" Mathi asks Aurelia with large, puppy-dog eyes.

She gives him a look of pure and utter contempt as we wait for the portal to be opened back to Caeli. Yup. My best friend hasn't changed one bit. The tension in the room, however, has, now that I've officially been announced as the last trial's winner. With so many death glares sliding my way, some indiscreetly, I all but pray to the Mother to open the damn portal quickly.

Come on, come on, come on.

I glance behind me at the four white wolves and beyond that to the door, where the others are returning to their packs. I couldn't be happier to get the hell out of Stormfire and away from Rizor... but I know my visits with Eziel are cut short. Caspian and Alaric feel so far away now, and I know, as much as Mathi isn't as domineering and controlling as Rizor, he still won't let me see them. I'm still a power piece for him.

I'm his to own for a week. My wolf itches to break free and rip the smug asshole to pieces. She always wanted to, but now I'm on her wavelength, and it's much harder to resist the urge.

"No," she sneers, looking over her shoulder at me. Things are so tense between us. The last time we spoke, I hurt her by just being there and she hurt me by accusing me of shit I didn't do on purpose. But I know why she did it, and I couldn't imagine how I'd react being as hurt as she was in that moment. I know she's sorry. I could see it right after she acted out.

By Mathi wanting to join the trials for my hand, to be my mate and own my power, he betrayed her, using me to do so, and I had no choice but to watch her heart break into pieces. I can't even blame her for hating me. Yet as I meet her ice-blue eyes, I see something else. Not hate, not anymore, but a softness she always had before for me. Aurelia was the only wolf in the pack who never once treated me like an outcast, and she saved me on more than one occasion. Forgiveness is a kindness, as Mum used to say. "I have wine, bad eighties music I love, and cake in my room. You in?"

"Hell, yes," I mutter, joy filling my chest, walking to her side. I could almost cry in relief, and I held myself together because too many wolves were watching. Alpha Mathi grumbles at us both before walking through the portal, and I go through with Aurelia, coming out onto the balcony of the alpha's home, the wisp of snow air blowing across my skin. I breathe it in, how this place was my home for so long and the memories of my family still haunt me. Aurelia is silent as I let her arm go and walk to the balcony edge, holding on to the pillar and looking over the snowy forest, the fields of white snow and ice, the mountains hanging over us all. It's bitterly cold and my tears feel frozen as I take in everything in front of me. So many memories come back to me, one in particular sticking to my mind. My mum had brought me to the alpha's house, along with all the children of my age, to celebrate the Mother by making ribbons into wolves and hanging them on all our doors. But I wasn't invited, and I was so upset. I still remember her taking me home, spending hours making the biggest wolf from ribbon and hanging it on our door.

We shifted and sang to the Mother under the moon that night and I swear she replied.

She always made sure I wasn't left out, that the pack couldn't make me feel any less wanted.

My mum, who made this pack feel warm, is gone, and I feel her loss.

"I miss her too," Aurelia whispers. "She truly was a wonderful wolf, and the pack lost a great woman that terrible day."

"They did," I agree, my voice lost. Aurelia comes to my side, sucking in a deep breath.

"I'm so fucking sorry I've been a bitch to you," she admits. "All I've ever wanted was to be alpha female, to make a real change to this pack for the better, and I thought he loved me. I loved him... but it wasn't real if he could throw me away for you. The idea of you and the power you could give him. He was using me, and I was so angry I couldn't see it had nothing to do with you. The whole competition is a joke, and I hope you win it. I'm on your side, and if you make a new pack, I'm signing up. Fuck Mathi and his stupidly nice body."

I meet her gaze, trying not to chuckle. "Thank you, and I understood you. I'm sorry he is a fucking idiot. You're stunning, funny and any wolf would be lucky to have you. He's a tool."

"Mother above, you're a saint. I'd hate me if I were you." She sadly laughs.

I knock her shoulder with my own. "I love you, what can I say? You had me at wine and cake."

She laughs sweetly this time. "Come on, let's get inside. It's cold as hell. Well, actually not, but you know what I mean."

Aurelia wraps her arm around my shoulders, and I sigh, letting her lead me inside the building. The wood walls seem older and less daunting than they did when I was last here and in the middle of the room, my brother is waiting by the fire.

The orange glow makes Leo's white hair seem golden, matching the gold tie he is wearing with his tux. He did always have bad choices in clothing and we never knew where he got it from. His eyes meet mine across the room like pits of brown coal on fire.

"Alpha Mathi caught me up on what happened. Congrats on your point, sister," he says, walking over to me and pulling me into a tight embrace. "You all right?"

"Coping," I admit, holding him back. This feels more like the brother I used to know. I pull back to look at him. "Look, Caspian, he—"

"Kissed you. My *sister*," Leo growls, his eyes turning white as his wolf. "I wouldn't suggest talking about my ex-best friend."

"No," I state, putting my hands on my hips as I step back. "Caspian Hardling risked his life, several times, to save me. I turned up on his door, homeless and alone, and he let me in at great risk to himself."

I'm not going to mention he tried to shut the door on me.

"I would be dead if it weren't for him, and yes, he kissed me, yes, I feel more than I can explain for him, but he is a good man. A good wolf and your closest friend. Don't judge him."

He glares at me in the same way he did when we were kids before Aurelia clears her throat. "Sorry to interrupt, but Lil has just fought in a trial. She looks and smells like shit and clearly needs a break. Do this tomorrow."

"Fine," he growls out and pauses to look down at me, speaking softer. "Come to the house tomorrow and I can show you Mum's gravestone. Okay?"

"Okay," I whisper.

Seeing the gravestone will make it real and part of me dreads going to see it. I hug him before he leaves, and Aurelia guides me to the back of the house and into her room. As she sorts out the music, I smile at my favourite wine on her dressing table and the huge chocolate cake next to it.

"Help yourself," Aurelia tells me. "And then you're going to tell me everything that has happened since you had to leave Caeli. Including the hot as fuck Caspian Hardling who apparently kissed you!"

"He wasn't the only one I've kissed," I laugh as I grab the wine and sit down on the small brown sofa at the end of her bed, crossing my legs. My best friend grabs the cake and as I start telling her everything, I breathe for the first time in a week.

Aurelia, cake, and wine was just what I needed.

CHAPTER 10

*O*ne thing I really haven't missed about home is all the snow.

My teeth chatter unrestrainedly as I follow a step or so behind Caspian up the driveway to my childhood home. Our boots crunch on the freshly fallen snow and the air nips at my rosy cheeks. Without even saying anything, Caspian falls into step with me and takes my hand. Using his demon abilities, he transfers warmth from his body into my own, and it spreads through me like a wave.

"Thank you," I say with an unexpectedly bashful smile. "I'm glad you left Dragon home. She'd hate all this snow."

Caspian laughs under his breath, forming a cloud of smoke in the air. "And Knight. Dragon and Knight were sunbathing in Ana's terrarium before I left."

Distracting myself from the building looming in the near distance, I ask, "Will they be safe with Annastasia? She didn't really come across the animal—err, demon—lover type."

"That's because she's half demon herself," he replies, still holding my hand. "She really knows how to handle fledglings, and just how much of a cute pain in the ass they can be."

I stop momentarily, taking his words in. "You know what, that actually makes so much sense. Did you see her at Dyenasty? Girl knows how to fight. Not to mention her intense aura and the way she..."

My mouth goes dry at the sight of my home, so close to me and yet so far. Everything's just as I left it, except for the fresh tracks in the driveway. They circle the house and disappear around the back. Caspian stops at the porch and the sun reflects off the huge icicles dangling from the gutter.

"Leo's waiting for you in the garden," Caspian says. "I'll wait inside."

Although I'd rather he came with me, I figure it's best that he doesn't. Leo's already tense about me being with someone he clearly now hates.

"Take this with you."

I glance up at Caspian as he removes his coat. He drapes it over my own, and I hug it close to me, breathing in his familiar scent. It's so comforting.

"I'll be right here, songbird," he whispers in my ear.

I press onto my tiptoes and steal a kiss from him. "Thank you, Cas."

When I move to walk away, he pulls me back to him and crushes his lips to mine once more. A burst of energy flares through me, setting my body ablaze with desire, and for a moment I'm able to forget what waits for me around the corner. Right now, it's just me and him, and nothing else.

A bird swooping from one tree to another tears us from each other's arms. Snow flutters from the branches to the ground as Caspian nods, taps my nose jokingly, and turns to make his way inside my home.

My home.

I don't think that place was ever truly my home. If it weren't for my mum and Leo, it would've been more like a prison.

I drag my attention from the house and shake my head in an effort to banish unpleasant memories. Pulling Caspian's warm coat tighter around me, I wade through the untouched snow toward the garden.

Everything is blanketed in a sea of snow and the only things detectable are my dad's work shed and a huge tree by the fence at the bottom. A shadow hangs underneath it. I take a deep, calming breath and walk towards it.

Leo doesn't look up at the sound of my footsteps. His gaze remains fixed on the bouquet of flowers resting against a beautiful headstone. The colourful petals are a stark contrast against the charcoal granite.

Here lies Zarina Thornblood.

Mother. Mate.

The bravest wolf who saved her child with her own life.

Always missed and forever loved.

Tears well in my eyes at the picture of her carved into the stone. She's sitting under this very tree and she's wearing the bracelet she gave me. I instinctively caress the bracelet on my wrist and fight the tears clawing to spill from my lashes.

"Mum used to bring us here when we were kids," Leo says, breaking the painful silence. "Do you remember that time you got stuck up this tree?"

I huff at him, more a breathy laugh through my nose than anything. "I remember the time you tricked me into climbing it. You said there was ancient magic carved into the heart of the tree, and that if I left a tooth in the hollow, the goddess would turn it into gold for me." A smile stretches my lips. "I broke my arm trying to get down. Lost another tooth for my effort."

My brother laughs quietly. "Mum nearly killed me that day."

I shrug at him. "Yeah, but my tooth did turn into gold," I reply, still grinning. "I knew it was you who left the trinket in the tree the next morning. You felt bad for me."

Not one for overly emotional stuff, my brother shrugs. "You were easier to get along with back then," he says after a moment. "And my friends weren't sniffing around you, either."

I know the remark is directed at Caspian, who can probably hear us even from way over here. It causes me to glance at the house, but there's no movement in the light bleeding through the kitchen window.

"Caspian's a good guy, Leo." I turn back to him. "He cares for me."

Leo shakes his head. "I doubt you'd say that if you knew what his kind are capable of."

I frown and narrow my eyes slightly. "But you work for one and you seem happy doing that."

He scoffs. "I'm as stuck down there as you are competing in the trials. I never wanted any of this to happen." He looks at me and then back to our mum's gravestone. His eyes gleam with scarcely restrained tears. He sniffs to hide his display of emotion. "If only I were there that day. Maybe Mum wouldn't have died. Maybe... maybe I could've helped you."

A shiver runs through me and it's not from the cold. When I first saw him again, I thought he was nothing more than a whipped lapdog. But all this time he's been beating himself up.

"Even if you were there," I say quietly, "there was nothing you could've done. Rizor wanted me. If anything, I'm to blame for Mum's death, not you."

Saying those words out loud catches me off guard for a moment. A tear escapes from my lashes and slips down my cheek. I don't wipe its track away and instead look at my mum's portrait.

"It was me she was trying to protect," I finish in a cracked voice. "So if you want to blame anyone, blame me."

Leo looks hard at me. "Stop that shit right now and listen to me. The only fuckers to blame here are Rizor and Dad. You're right that even if I

G. BAILEY & SCARLETT SNOW

were there when this went down, they'd still have betrayed our family. But... I at least would've felt better knowing I laid into them a little."

I smile at his grin and wipe my eyes. "What happened to Dad's body?"

His expression darkens, and he turns back to the gravestone. "He didn't deserve to be buried here. Your little prince, Eziel, threw him into Hell's Coctyus river where he belongs."

I nod and bite my lip, refraining from speaking ill of the dead. In some packs it's considered bad luck. However, Leo does have a point. If anyone's to blame, it is my dad and Rizor, and all those who helped them along the way. As far as I'm concerned, my dad got what he deserved in the end, and so will Rizor once I'm through with him. Too bad I can't throw Rizor into the lake of ice, either.

The chilly air sweeps over me again, dragging my hair over my shoulder. I place my hand on the top of the headstone and close my eyes. *I love you, Mum, and no matter what, I will avenge you. I promise.*

It feels like only seconds I stand there, but when I open my eyes, my fingers are numb from the cold.

"C'mon, Lil." My brother nods over his shoulder. "Judging by that smell, someone's got some hot chocolate waiting for you inside."

We walk through the garden side by side, just like we used to do as kids.

"Are you coming inside?" I ask quietly.

Leo stares at the house for a moment, then shakes his head. "I've already said my goodbyes." He trains his focus back on me. "You should do the same, Lil. And hey, if letting go of the past means creating memories with people I'd prefer you didn't, so be it. You deserve to be happy… and to win the trials."

He winks at me and then leaves before I'm able to process my reply. His words stick with me though, and I follow where his line of sight had strayed to moments ago. My breath hitches at the sight of my guys waiting for me. Eziel sits on the second last stair and tosses a snowball between his hands. Behind him, Alaric swings on my mum's bench while Caspian leans against the porch, his arms crossed.

All three of them look up at the same moment.

Alaric stops swinging and jumps down the steps, but it's Eziel who reaches me first. He wears the same worried expression as the one he wore when he found me in Alaric's bed.

"Hey," I say quietly.

The edge of his mouth twitches in a smile. "Hey."

Alaric appears beside us. "Come hither, my young lady, to where a grand surprise awaits you."

He loops my arm through his and gently steers me into the house. I smile weakly at him and the grin he slides at me causes my heart to skip a beat. He's up to something, but what? I glance over my shoulder to make sure my other guys are following suit. They're both exchanging an amused grin, which tells me whatever Alaric has arranged for me, they're in on it too.

I take a long, quiet inhale through my nose, and allow myself to be guided into my home.

The heat from the kitchen warms my cheeks and the scents from my childhood wrap around me like a warm, familiar blanket. This is where everything changed.

My life. My family. My future.

I can still see Rizor standing by the door with my mum held terrified in his arms.

It's with tremendous effort I manage to hold back my tears. I don't want to cry in front of my guys. They've clearly come here to support me.

However, when my gaze lands on the table, a solitary tear slips from my lashes.

Alaric stops us beside it and nods proudly to the birthday cake. "Made it myself. Dark Belgian chocolate with a white-chocolate, raspberry frosting. Triple layered."

Caspian slides down onto a chair. "It's all he's talked about since this morning."

The Rivermare glares at him, but his attention is drawn back to me when I open my mouth.

"It looks delicious," I say, smiling at him and then down at the cake. "Who's it for?"

The fact that I don't know his or Eziel's birthday embarrasses me, and my cheeks flame under their perusal. I know this can't be for Caspian because I'm pretty sure his birthday is closer to Leo's which is around Christmastime.

Caspian shakes his head. "Told you she'd forget." He looks at me. "Today is your birthday, songbird. Now let's light these bad boys and make a wish."

He tosses Alaric a lighter, who starts to ignite each of the candles. I count nineteen of them in total. Now the heat assaulting my cheeks is directed at myself. I've been so caught up in survival that I completely forgot about my own birthday. It's always been something I enjoyed in the past. Mum always made such a big deal out of it. I wonder if that's why Leo asked me to come today. Did he know about this surprise?

The thought pulls me back to reality. When I look at the cake again, the candles have been lit, and the guys start singing happy birthday. My face heats up again, partly from embarrassment, but the other part is because of how sweet they're being.

Their voices and kindness unlock something inside me. It's as if they just unplugged the dam that's been bursting at the seams ever since my world was turned upside down.

"This was a stupid idea," I hear Caspian say over my quiet sobs. "Fuck, I shouldn't have said anything," he grumbles.

"N—no, it's not—not what you think," I hurriedly explain, but I allow the tears to continue falling. "It's just… you have no idea how much this means to me." I wipe my eyes with both hands and laugh sheepishly. "I never realised how much I needed it."

'It' being my guys around me. How can I be so happy when there's been so much death, so much betrayal and havoc, taking place around me?

Eziel reaches for my chin and slowly lifts my head. His eyes search my own as if seeking answers to the questions I'm not yet brave enough to voice out loud. There's a side of me that's ashamed to admit how happy I am with them. Even on my birthday, it's surely no excuse.

"What are you thinking?" he whispers.

My answer is similarly whispered, though it's threaded with pain that claws between the cracks. "I'm thinking I have no right to feel happy like this… especially not in the place he killed her." Instinctively I cast a glance around the room and my stomach clenches as an icy chill sweeps through me. "My mum died trying to save me. In this very house. The only time I should feel happy again is when I'm dancing on Rizor's grave."

A brief silence, heavy with my guilt and pain, oscillates between us for what feels like an eternally long moment. But then Alaric's voice breaks it like a shattered mirror, firm and resolute.

"That's where you're wrong. You deserve to be happy after all the bullshit you've gone through. I know that." He flicks his chin briefly at the others. "They know that." His gaze cuts back to me and there's an intenseness within it that seizes my breath. "You know that. Now, as for dancing on that sonuvabitch's grave? That's payback and I'll be dancing right there with you," he adds with a wink.

I chuckle despite my inner turmoil.

Caspian nods with a grin. "What he said."

Brushing his thumb across my cheek, Eziel steers me back to him. "So let yourself be happy, even if it's just for a few minutes, and take comfort in the fact that my father can't stand it." His thumb strays upward to my eye, and he brushes away a lingering tear. "He thought he could break you in that dungeon, Lilith. The fact that he couldn't meant he had to admit that he has no power over you. That *you're* more powerful than *him*. And then you being happy?" His lips tilt in a smirk. "Now that's just plain old rubbing salt in the wound."

Over his shoulder, Caspian dips a finger into the side of the cake and licks it. "Speaking of salt..." He grimaces at Alaric. "Did you forget to add the sugar, mate?"

I've never seen Alaric move so fast in my life.

He lunges for the table, picks up a teaspoon, and swipes the frosting. His expression twists into a grimace.

"Mother. Fucker!"

We all burst out laughing which in turn makes Alaric laugh, too. It's deeper than the others, and it sends a shiver through me.

Caspian pats him on the shoulder. "Fear not, Big Guy. I already picked up a cake the other night." He glances at me and nods. "We can have another celebration once we're all back home."

"Pretty sure the cake won't be edible by then," Eziel counters.

Caspian waves a hand dismissively. "It'll be fine. I froze it."

His reply causes Alaric to choke on something. A dark look shadows his features as he stands from the table.

"Where are you going?" I ask.

Alaric pulls a crimson cloak off the back of his chair and drapes it over his broad shoulders.

"To get my bake on," he replies. "Because like fuck am I letting a half demon outshine me with some frozen shit."

"Triple chocolate frozen shit," Caspian counters. Alaric winks and ruffles my hair playfully as he opens the door, but he pauses when Caspian's voice catches him before he leaves. "And don't forget to wear your frilly pink apron this time. Wouldn't want that fancy cloak of yours to get dirty."

"Fuck you," comes the Rivermare's reply.

It's accompanied by two middle fingers raised high in the air as Alaric storms outside. The door barely closes when Eziel makes a move to follow him.

"You're going too?" I ask, unable to restrain the frown that creeps onto my face. "I mean, you just got here."

"Yeah but my invite only extends so long." His brows draw together in a barely suppressed grimace. "We were lucky that Caeli asshole approved our visit in the first place. I almost resorted to a different method of persuasion until a friend of yours, Aurelia, stepped in and convinced him to let us stay an hour."

He shoots me that familiar lopsided grin, the same one he wore the day I first met him slouched on his throne as though he were the only prince in existence. "Besides, her methods involved much less bloodshed. Also it only cost me a bottle of wine for my trouble."

"Yeah, that sounds like Aurelia." I return his smile in an effort to hide my disappointment at him leaving. "I'm glad she helped get you here. I just wish you and Alaric could've stayed longer."

Eziel must sense the disappointment in my voice. In two long strides, he closes the distance between us and gently slides his fingers down my arm.

"Take as much time as you need here," he whispers, moving down to the ring he placed on my finger, "and remember that I'm always here."

He tilts my jaw and stares intently into my eyes. Just when I think he's about to kiss me on the mouth, at the last second he lifts his head and presses his lips to my forehead just as I close my lids. Eziel lingers for a moment and my skin flares where his flesh touches mine, a whisper of a caress. But when I open my eyes again, he's gone although his kiss remains committed to my memory.

The door closes, the soft click of it falling into place bringing me back to reality. Across the table, Caspian stares at me with an intense longing in his gaze I've never seen present before. It's almost… possessive.

Jealous even.

In a series of blurred movements, he's taking me in his arms, anchoring my legs around his waist and setting me on the edge of the table. His tongue spears my lips and enters my mouth in an almost wild frenzy, as if his succubus side has been unleashed and he's no longer trying to hold him at bay. This side to him is as intoxicating as all his others, if not more.

"Are you only being this nice to me because it's my birthday?" I whisper.

He smirks at me. "I'm only being this nice to you because I'm not holding back anymore." He kisses me, stealing every sensation tingling through my body. "All this time, I've tried fighting it... tried depriving myself of the one thing I've ever wanted."

Another kiss; this time, slow and gentle.

Even though I'm certain I know the answer, I ask teasingly, "And what *do* you want, Mr Harding?"

A wry grin stretches over his lips. "You. And I'll be damned if I'm gonna sit here and watch Ez and Alaric kiss you unless I'm kissing you, too."

The air is quite literally sucked out from my lungs when he claims my mouth again. Only this time, there's an explosion that sears through my whole body the instant our lips lock.

"It's only ever been you, songbird," he murmurs against me.

His hand slides over my breast and he lightly squeezes, dragging a moan out from me. But the reality of what we're about to do in the last place I saw my mum causes me to withdraw.

"Wait, not… not in here."

He pulls back to look at me, his lips swollen and pupils fully dilated. "All right, birthday girl. We can just go to sleep. I'll even hitch up in Leo's old room, give you some space."

When he tries to turn away, I catch his hand and pull him back.

"No, that's not what I mean. I want this." My cheeks burn as I peer unexpectedly coyly through my lashes at him. "I want you, Cas. I've always wanted you. But I don't want our first time to be in the place where Rizor…"

I trail off, unable to finish my sentence, but Caspian quickly catches on. He nods and lifts me off the table, setting me on the ground. He then lightly caresses the side of my face, and I lean into him, briefly closing my eyes and breathing in his scent.

"When you're ready, songbird," he whispers. "I'm not going anywhere."

My heart skips a beat, and I look up at him with a smile full of adoration for his patience and understanding.

"You know something? This has been one of my best birthdays yet." I gesture to Alaric's abomination on the table. "Salted cake included."

He ruffles my hair affectionately. "You're always so easily pleased."

"That I am. What do you say we watch *Frozen* before the trial starts?"

He raises a brow. "Well, it is your birthday, so I'll surrender this one time."

I tap his arm in playful admonishment. "Don't act like you're not delighted. I know you secretly love Disney, almost as much as Alaric does baking. Hmm. I wonder what the prince's guilty pleasure is...'"

Caspian chuckles. "You wouldn't think it looking at him, but he's a sucker for romance books, especially historical ones. He has a whole shelf filled in his room."

I blink for several moments, completely taken aback by this information, then I grab Caspian and steer him towards the living room. "You're going to tell me *everything*."

Caspian smiles, a genuine one that lights up his eyes. "He did mention the words 'bodice rippers' once, whatever the fuck that means."

"*What*?!" I let out a surprised, delighted squeal. "I love reading those! I can't believe it… I have a baker, a Disney lover, *and* a bookworm for my lovers. I'm officially the luckiest girl in the world."

"No," I hear him murmur as I drag him into the living room. "We're the lucky ones."

CHAPTER 11

The chilly wind blows my grey fur-lined cloak around my legs as I stand on the balcony, next to Aurelia and Alpha Mathi, as several portals open at the same time. Every single one of them are different and unusual. These trials will go down in history and the Caeli pack is out here, recording and watching. In front of the alpha's house are rows of snowmobiles, ready to take us to wherever this test is. I wrap my hand around the daggers attached to my hips, given to me by Aurelia late last night. I know she hates that she can't come today, but coming to the Caeli pack feels like the closure I desperately needed.

Alaric appears first, wearing a long, dark, midnight-blue cloak over thick leather clothes, strapped with magical weapons. He looks right up at me, and I nod once, letting him know I'm okay; this time, we have no choice but to wear the damn cloaks. Eziel and Rizor appear next, both in leather and looking more related than ever before. The Terraseeker alpha is followed by Lord Dyrk and Caspian, and the portals close shut behind them.

Alpha Mathi steps forward. They only make the building tension worse when he starts talking by outright ignoring him or looking bored.

"Welcome to the grand Caeli pack," he starts. *Grand? What a load of*— "The second trial awaits, and it is being held in an area called the Autem Latus."

My blood goes cold, and I glance at Aurelia, who looks shocked. She didn't know. Alpha Mathi has lost his goddamn mind. The Autem Latus is a place of horrid creatures, locked away for a reason. Ice Wraiths. They eat wolves and humans like sport. Nearly half the Caeli pack was killed over a thousand years ago, locking those things away under the tallest mountain. The first alpha of Caeli was born in the ash and burning dust of this mountain pack and the very few people left within it. "The Autem Latus is an upside down world and all rules are backwards. To gain a point, you must take the crystal dagger from the head of an ice wraith."

I'm so fucked.

I don't let my expression change, let anyone sense the creeping fear, but when I catch Alaric's eyes, I know he sees it. "Take a snowmobile. The trial will begin when I open the door to the Autem Latus."

Rizor smirks at me as I turn to Aurelia and she embraces me tightly, whispering in my ear. "My mum used to sing songs to me about the ice wraiths and she told me they love music. Sing for them."

One problem, I'm a terrible singer.

Aurelia knows this, but I thank her with my eyes before walking down the steps. Alaric waits for me at the bottom and bows his head. I do the same. "Ride with me?"

"Always," I say, truthfully, meaningfully. I missed him, and being away from Alaric, Caspian, and Eziel has only made my emotions that more real.

And unavoidable. Alaric smiles as I take his waiting hand and he guides me over to the snowmobile, climbing on board. I slide in front of him, and he wraps an arm around my waist, pulling me back on the seat so my ass is pressed against him.

"Ah, such good memories in this pack. It's where we first met, wasn't it, Lilith?" Rizor calls over.

A deep growl vibrates from my chest as I sneer at him. "I hope your balls freeze off, Rizor."

He glowers at me and I turn away, hearing Alaric's deep laugh vibrating against my chest. His hot breath blows against my hair as he turns the engine on, and I look over to the snowmobile next to us with Eziel climbing on board.

"Lilith. Lyulf." He nods to us, a secret smile on his lips as he turns his snowmobile on. "Be careful."

"I will," I tell him just before he takes off. Alaric reverses our snowmobile out before speeding off down the snow trial, after the others. I hold on to the small bend of the snowmobile in front of me as Alaric drives us over hills of snow and into the marked tracks to the mountains. As we drive, I run every book, story, or even mention of the ice wraiths over in my mind to find something to help us. A lot of them do say music and the ice wraiths are linked, but can't be any song or melody to soothe them. They said the female sang a song sent to her by the Mother and guided them away from the remaining village, saving so many, and even then she died in the end. The Mother isn't here to help me right now, though. Alaric presses a kiss on the top of my head, no doubt feeling my anxiety and panic about this. The last trial was brutal, near un-survivable and this is just worse. I doubt luck is going to help, but I'm going to try my hardest to get a point. I'm not being sold to the highest bidder.

The mountain casts a dark shadow over us as we drive into the base, stopping the snowmobile outside and walking to the door of the mountain. The door is ancient, filled with written Latin warnings not to enter, to never go inside, to be wary. Of course, this doesn't stop Alpha Mathi from unlocking the door with a giant key and walking inside. Alaric takes my hand as we head inside, onto a rocky ledge, blue light glowing from deep within. The ledge hangs upside down, like all of the paths and jagged ice, and there are even outlines of old houses in the ice which are wrongly placed. I walk closer to the edge and look down, seeing where the light is coming from. A river of blue ice glows as bright as a star and sleeping above it are ice wraiths, curled into skeleton fish bones. The door slams shut behind us, and I look over at Alaric as Caspian walks to me.

The others start making their way down the paths, and Eziel looks back at me once before going with his father. Keeping an eye on him in case the psychopath decides to betray us all.

"Songbird, any chance you know much about Ice Wraiths?"

"Nothing good or helpful," I admit, just as we all hear the ear-splitting sound of bones cracking and crunching. I look down and instead of seeing sleeping Ice Wraiths, they have gone. I barely get to open my mouth to warn Alaric when one of them crashes into the rock under our feet and smashes it to pieces. I'm flung into the air, my hand slipping from Alaric's, and I scream as I free fall, spinning in the air. I hear a growl right before something warm crashes into me, slamming us both into a cavern space. The dirt and ice cut through my arms as I roll to a stop and look over at the red wolf panting, limping as he crawls to me.

Eziel.

"You saved me?" I whisper to him, and he whines as he pushes his head against my arm, telling me to get up. Groaning, I pick myself up, ignoring the screaming pain in my ribs and back. My eyes go wide and I rush to the edge. "Alaric! Caspian!"

No one replies to me, so I search around, seeing nothing. Then I hear Eziel shifting, and I turn back, trying not to stare at his very naked, and stunningly perfect, body.

"Wow. I mean..." I blush, clearing my throat, and meet his eyes. "Are you okay?"

"My leg is broken. Are you okay?"

"I'm fine. Thank you for saving me," I add softly. "That was a huge risk for yourself."

He shrugs. "I didn't, and would never, see it that way. Rizor has his point and so do I. Take it."

He holds up the glowing blue dagger made of bone and crystal.

I shake my head. "No, I will earn my own. I have to. Get out of here, Eziel."

"Not without you," he replies with a frown, curling his hands into fists. "You never listen to me, Lilith, and I'm telling you to save your own ass. Just this once. I won't see you fucking killed over this."

"You will see me win, and I will see you leave. You're hurt," I demand.

He limps over to me, clutching my upper shoulders, staring into my eyes. "Lilith, I'm not leaving without you. Ever. I made my choice when we met and I looked into your eyes. I saw the brightest and most dangerous fire lurking there, and I will happily burn for you. I always have done."

Eziel leans down and kisses me, shushing all my screaming internal thoughts. His lips are gentle, erotic, and soft as he kisses me, like he wants to take his time. I press myself closer, hyper aware he is naked even more when something hard presses into my stomach. The sound of the wraith moving around makes me snap out of it and step back.

"Shift back and we need to get moving, Prince," I say with a small smile.

He grins before shifting into his red wolf. I slide a dagger out of my thigh clasp and walk out of the cavern, almost balancing on the upside-down steps. Three wraiths fly around in the air in a formation, and it takes me a second to realise one of them has someone on top of it. Alaric. He is riding the giant fish shaped wraith—made of pure bones—like a horse. I catch the smile and insanely amused glint in his eyes as he rips off his dagger and then jumps off the wraith as it collapses into bones that fall to the bottom of the cavern.

Badass alpha vibes.

"Lilith!" Caspian shouts, and I follow his voice to see him on the bottom floor, bleeding and looking rough but alive. Relieved, I turn my gaze to the wraiths to see all three of them have paused, and they are looking down at Caspian.

Fear, like nothing I've ever felt, smacks into my chest as they begin to fly down towards him in formation.

"Cas!" I scream, rushing to the edge, helpless to do anything but watch. Eziel howls from my side as I scream, trying to get them to notice me instead. But they are focused on Cas. He runs to the back of the ice river, scratching at the ice walls to try to climb out, but he is trapped. There isn't a way out of this.

Sing. Sing with me.

Without thinking about who the voice is, I open my mouth and sing a song I've never heard in my life. The words come to me as my body warms and my feet leave the ground. I can't see anything but red and white power blasting out of my body, along with the enchanting song. I've never been able to hold a note in my life, but the song that comes out of my lips, in a language I don't know, is beautiful. The wraiths pause and spin around, looking up at me with nothing but bottomless bone pits where eyes once were. They fly to me quickly, daunting and huge as they sway to my voice, like snakes in a trance. I reach out and pull out the dagger from the wraith in front of me, and it collapses into a pile of dead bones. I go to the next one and do the same, watching it collapse. As the last note leaves my lips, the final wraith lets out a hallowing noise and shoots up into the cavern and out of sight. I collapse onto the ground with a thud, feeling drained and empty in a pile of bones.

"I've got you," Alaric says, picking me up off the ground and into his arms. I clutch the daggers, my two points, to my chest as I fall into a deep sleep.

CHAPTER 12

"*A*re you sure you're all right to travel?" Aurelia asks me once again, ignoring the crying and whining of Mathi.

Poor little alpha puppy lost his arm to one of the wraiths. He should be thankful he's already started healing. He was dragged out of the cave by Caspian, who felt bad for him, but he was too late to save his arm. Apparently, he had it ripped off right before I started singing.

Too late to help him. Shucks.

A wolf missing an arm, a leg when shifted, is going to be challenged for alpha position and I'm sure he knows it. The other alphas, Caspian, Lord

Dyrk, and Eziel, were commanded to leave as soon as they came out of the cavern.

My ribs ache, I have one hell of a headache, and I'm tired, but I know the Terraseeker alpha is waiting outside for me. I finish pulling on the soft, cream cashmere cardigan over a black tee shirt and skinny jeans. I slide my fluffy socks into my boots and slip my dagger from Alaric's mother's collection into it.

It turns out Caspian, Alaric, Eziel, Rizor and the Terraseeker alpha got their daggers, but I was the one who won by getting two of them. It means I'm higher on the board of these trials, and no matter how crappy I feel, I can't help but smile. The daggers are all being kept in the Caeli pack museum as they are dangerous objects to have, much like the library of books they have here. Caeli, the pack who protects knowledge, has always been seen as a weak pack, but truthfully that was never right. The knowledge this pack has could destroy the world quicker than the brutal strength of the Stormfire pack.

"I'm good," I tell her, leaving the medical bay in the alpha's house as quick as I can before Aurelia never lets me leave.

I feel the building tension in this pack, and part of me worries about a new alpha being in charge of this place, of Aurelia. I'm sure she can handle her own if that happens. I thank the healer wolf before going to the entrance hall where the Terraseeker alpha is waiting. He is watching the fire, silent and daunting with his tall, seven-foot frame.

"I don't believe we have been formally introduced. I am Alpha Eldridge of the Terraseeker pack," he says, turning to face me with a bow. "I am a wolf of little words, but I wish to leave this pack. If you are able."

"Yes," I reply as his dark, deep brown eyes fall on me. "I'm completely able."

He seems perfectly kind and that pretense—because it *is* a pretense—makes my skin crawl. Somehow, this lanky and strongly built wolf is an alpha, and the glowing green gemstone around his neck reminds me of that fact. He is good at sweet talking and appearances.

Maybe all Terraseeker wolves are. I have had little interaction with them.

"There is a portal outside," Aurelia says, inclining her head to Alpha Eldridge and touching my arm gently. "I expect to see you soon. I might not be alpha female, but my door, this pack's door, is open for you. I vow it."

I embrace her tightly for just a second. "I vow you alone will always have my support."

Aurelia's water glazed eyes meet mine before I turn away and walk out of the cabin and to Alpha Eldridge's side as an emerald portal appears. It is a wave of leaves, green and vibrant, like the fur of the Terraseeker wolves I can see on the other side. I walk through first and step out from blistering cold to a mildly warm breeze that blows pink blossoms past my eyes. The sweet scent fills my senses quite pleasantly.

The Terraseeker pack is an explosion of green fields, blossom trees, tall hills of straw fields and trees for miles to see, all of it stunning to look at. The sun is bright in the sky, the air humid and thick, the breeze a welcome brush against my heating skin. The woodland is to our left, and in the trees are houses built from stone and wood that tower into the sky. Huge wolves with dark green fur, and wolves in their human form, cross the bridges and stairs that connect the buildings.

"It's beautiful," I admit as Alpha Eldridge stops at my side. I hate to admit it, but I used to sleep through the lessons on this pack and its traditions as I found all of it boring. I wanted to be fighting and training instead of reading books on other packs. Now I wish I listened. There's so much about this pack I don't know.

One of the five Terraseeker wolves shifts back, and my eyes go wide.

"Annastasia?"

She inclines her head, a wave of black hair concealing her body. She doesn't look any different from when we last saw each other, hunting the level five demon back at Dyenasty. I never saw her much, but I admired her fighting skills and respected her for those alone. She had my back in there and didn't run. Not many would have done that.

Her emerald eyes flash briefly at me before sharply turning to the alpha. She holds her back rigidly straight. "Alpha Eldridge, permission to speak?"

I try not to bristle at the fact she needs permission to speak to me.

"Are females not allowed to speak without permission in this pack?" I ask dryly.

"You know little of our ways, young female alpha," Alpha Eldridge replies. "The Terraseeker pack was created by the Mother to conceal and protect the humans from knowledge of our existence. We protect, we keep secrets, and we learn when it is the right time to speak and when it is not. Females must ask for permission to speak to outsiders because every word could put our existence at risk. Annastasia was asking permission to speak with you, as will every member of my pack, or I will have their tongue."

I grit my teeth and hold the alpha's gaze, not caring how defiant he might find me. He growls low as he turns to Annastasia. "Yes, female, you may speak with her and show her around."

With that, the alpha leaves with the other four wolves, and I wait until they are out of earshot. "Are Knight and Dragon with you?"

"Yes. You owe me for babysitting, and I watched you fight. I like to spar. Will you join me in your time here?"

I smile. "Yes, I would like that."

"Good." She nods formally. "Come."

I don't have much choice but to walk at her side across the green grass and straw field into the trees. Annastasia pauses every so often to tell me about the place as we walk under the first part of the pack houses in the trees, passing countless wolves who go silent when we are close. Alpha Eldridge has a tight grip on this pack. Eventually, we go up the steps and see the houses up close. There is a row of huts, made of wood and shaped into triangles with windows on the edges that no doubt look up at the sky, seeing the stars at night. Annastasia walks me down to the third one and opens the door. "They are in there. This hut is for you. Mine is next door."

"Can I ask why you were in the Demon Hunting Trials? I didn't know Terraseeker wolves were interested in demon hunting."

"To be blunt, I'm a spy for my alpha, trained from birth. The Stormfire pack had something interesting going on, and I was there to see what, or who, was causing a commotion." She clenches her jaw. "I was too late to prevent Dove's betrayal."

"Why did she betray us, anyway? Do you know?" I ask. "Being a trained spy and all."

She brushes her hair over her shoulder, still buck naked, and it's worse now that her hair doesn't cover up... things. "Yes, but if I tell you that, you will owe me."

I shrug. "Already do. I might as well owe you one more thing."

And I really do want to know. Or rather, need. I'm good at reading people. At least I thought I was, and I never thought Dove was evil. I didn't get that vibe from her at all, but there was something desperate about her actions that night.

Forced.

I didn't see pleasure in her eyes before I hit her.

I saw pain.

"Your funeral," she replies with a hint of a smile. "Dove has a sister who is currently locked away in Rizor's prison system. Dove has no other family and Rizor was bribing her to find you. I believe Dove didn't want to betray you and didn't know who you were until that final mission. It was when I realised as well. When you stopped that demon with your power."

Maybe I shouldn't have hit her so hard. "Thanks... have you seen Dove recently?"

"Yes, Caspian hired me to track her and lock her up. She is here, contained, and no you cannot see her without Caspian's permission. Unless you pay more than he does," she tells me.

Brutal and honest.

I want to see her but not yet, and I want to ask Caspian what he plans to do with her anyway, if he knows about her sister. I understand what she did, even if it still hurts. I'd do anything for my family. Betray, kill, steal. Whatever it would take for just one more day with my mum or brother... and others in my life. Love makes us desperate.

"I have no money," I admit.

"Shame. I like money almost as much as I like sparring. See you at five AM for that, by the way." She nods before walking away.

"Wait. Five *AM*?" I call after her. "Really?"

I hear her laugh before she shifts into her green wolf and runs off down the pathway. I shake my head, wondering if I actually like her before heading inside the hut, only to pause at the cutest sight. Dragon is wrapped around a yellow pillow, twice the size of when I last saw him, and next to his side, sitting upright against a grey sofa, is Knight, snoring lightly. I quietly shut the door, admiring the modern hut with three grey sofas, a green stained glass coffee table on top of yellow carpet. There is a small tv on the wall next to two pine doors and strange 3D paintings of forests and shadows on the walls. I sit down on the sofa, listening to them sleep for a few moments before Dragon opens his eyes, locking onto me. He uncurls from the pillow, knocking Knight off the sofa.

"What in the frigging hellish nightmare am I doing on the floor?!" Knight shouts as Dragon climbs onto my lap, and I stroke his head, hearing his purr-like noises.

"Hey, guys," I whisper, my voice clogged with emotion.

"Lilith?" Knight asks, jumping on the sofa. He grins at me, and I smile back. "You've come to save us from this pack and that black-haired witch! I thought red haired witches were the evil ones, but I was wrong! The black-haired witch is a vegetarian! Disgusting!"

I laugh, bursting into fits of giggles as Knight continues to rant about the many vegetables and terrible cooking skills Annastasia has.

Dragon looks up at me. *We are never leaving your side again, alpha queen of the wolves. The Mother sent us to you.*

"You can speak?" I blurt out.

"What? You didn't know?" Knight asks. "Dragon is a girl, apparently, and talks all of the time. The Mother this, the Mother that."

"Did the Mother actually send you both to me?"

Knight pauses, and for a moment, he looks serious. "Every alpha is sent a creature or two for help, if they so need it. We both didn't know what we were made for until we met you."

"And we failed," Dragon whispers into my mind. *"But not again."*

"You didn't fail anyone," I firmly tell them. "I'm glad you're here, and I do need your help. What do you think of the Terraseeker pack and its alpha?"

Knight jumps on my lap, resting an elbow on Dragon's back. "Total dickhead, that alpha. Control freak on crack."

"Yeah, I got that impression," I say with an amused grin. "Anything else?"

"The pack is silent. Can you hear anything? A child laugh? A bird cry?" Dragon's concerned voice echoes through my mind. *"No pack should be so silent. This pack is wrong."*

I sit quietly for a moment, and I realise she is right. I don't hear anything and that's not right. "I'm here for a week. I just need to stay alive that long."

"Alaric has appeared in the pack. I sense his presence close," Dragon says. *"Would you like me to guide him here?"*

I widen my eyes in surprise. "You can do that?"

"Yes," she replies simply. *"Dragons, such as I, are rare and precious for our power. And my power is yours for the kindness you gave me. We are family."*

"We are and always will be family, Dragon," I softly tell her. "By the way, do you have a name or do you like Dragon?"

"I like Dragon," she replies. *"The wolf is outside."*

"I'll get the door," Knight says and walks over to it, just before it's pushed open and Alaric saunters in, sending Knight flying across the room. He lands on one of the sofas with a crash and groans.

"Knight, are you okay?" I immediately get up to help him while he glares at Alaric who is shutting the door.

Alaric stops short and looks at Knight. "Shit. Sorry, little buddy. Didn't see you there."

Knight scoffs and hobbles onto his feet. "So you claim. You just want Lilith to yourself, don't you?" he demands.

Alaric runs his hand through his hair. "I have no desire to lock Lilith away and not let the world love her as many already do."

"How are you here? Does Alpha Eldridge know you're here?" I question.

"Are you not happy to see me?"

"No—"

"I'm joking," he teases, sitting next to me. "He knows I'm here and doesn't care too much. The Terraseeker pack has always been open for visitors."

"So you've been here before?"

"Twice. Despite what the world says about us, I did try to make alliances with other packs, but I had issues with the way Alpha Eldridge controls his people and changed my mind."

"It's weirdly silent."

"At night, it's even more silent. No one even moans during sex in this pack without the alpha knowing. It's creepy."

I chuckle at him. "And listening out for moans in the night from complete strangers isn't creepy? I didn't know you were the stalker type. Or just kinky like that," I tease, only half joking with him. Because I do want to know what he likes in that department and the idea of being just a spectator has never really gone through my mind before.

He grins and winks at me. "I like listening and watching all sorts of things, Lilith. Perhaps I can show you sometime. Let me corrupt you a little. I promise you'll enjoy it."

My cheeks feel like they're on fire. Knight, in comparison, pretends to be sick by dry retching.

"I'm still in the room! Ugh, my mind is burning with unerasable thoughts and images." He glares at us. "Be gone, the both of you!"

"You're so overdramatic," I mutter.

He huffs and turns away from me.

Alaric clears his throat. "How about I get some food? You can come with me if you want, Knight. I'll even buy whatever you want as an apology."

Knight turns back with a big smile on his face. "I always knew I liked you, alpha wolf. Let's go."

I chuckle as Alaric kisses the side of my head. "Food's always been the way to Knight's heart," I say.

He helps the little demon onto his shoulder. "Aye, I figured that, going by all the wrappers he left in your apartment."

"I was peckish," Knight states defensively. "Now, I hear these Terraseeker wolves are known for their seafood. Even more than your pack."

Alaric scoffs. "Where the hell did you hear that nonsense?"

"Never you mind. At any rate, it is a knight's job to know everything."

"Oh, is it now?" Alaric grins at me from over his shoulder and then opens the door. "Then tell me, little knight, where are you about to land in about three seconds if you don't shut up?"

Knight totally disregards the warning and starts going over an extensive shopping list that is definitely going to hurt Alaric's wallet. You can't help but laugh. They're so comical together.

"That wolf loves you, Lilith, and he is going to be your mate," Dragon says softly.

I only smile as I watch their retreat. "I know, Dragon, and it's not a bad thing. It's a blessing."

CHAPTER 13

*A*ll around me, demons, wolves, and wolves in human form wait with bated breath for the trial to begin. The forest stretches endlessly at the other side of the meadow. The trees are so tall the tips of them seem to touch the sky.

Alaric's wolf brushes his shoulder against my own, the glint in his eye akin to that of a smirk. I know that look of his. He's goading me to see who'll reach the forest first. Caspian and Eziel have already stated who'll win between me and Alaric. Apparently, they quite like my chances of outrunning a Rivermare alpha.

That's if they fail to outrun him first.

While he is the fastest out of our group, it won't stop me from trying.

"Since my pack is known to keep things short," the Terraseeker alpha announces. "I will say only this: *reap the flower that grows in stone*, and good luck."

Before he even finishes speaking, he shifts into his wolf and lunges for the forest.

Everyone takes off after him, including me. Growls, shrieks, roars, and hisses from various creatures echo around me. Wolves snap at each other's paws in a desperate attempt to thwart them. While a Caeli wolf pins a Stormfire wolf down on his back, I leap over them and the trees.

The scent of leaves, freshly washed in rain, engulfs my senses, and I take a deep breath of it.

I'll never get tired of this smell.

Another smell accompanies it, though why he's trying to hide from me I'll never know. Without even looking at Eziel, I break into a run again. He follows me swiftly through the towering trees, over the huge moss-covered rocks and collapsed trunks stretching out on the forest floor. My paws barely touch the ground as we run side by side, playfully pawing and biting each other.

I climb onto an ancient ruin and balance on the edge. Eziel runs alongside me as I trail the building carefully. Small stones scuttle under my paws when I push off, and they land on him… just before *I* land on him.

My victory is short-lived, however.

Eziel's wolf is stronger than mine, and he smoothly manages to pin me underneath him. Anyone else and I'd have challenged them. But with Eziel, I submit willingly; freely.

He stares into my eyes and then leans down to lick the side of my face. I catch his cheek with a lick before he pulls back, then we're taking off again.

I cut short when Alaric, half-dressed, blocks the path.

He places his hands on his hips and quirks a brow like a disapproving father would.

"Are you done playing now?"

I'm just about to nod when I realise Alaric is looking not at me but behind.

"Pay up, young prince."

Eziel shifts behind me and seconds later throws a metal object over my head. It sails past me towards Alaric, who catches it without even flinching.

"Told you our girl would beat you to the starting line." Alaric inspects the blade and nods his approval. "She damn near beat me. I'd never have lived it down back home."

He pulls on a shirt, followed by a belt of weapons, and equips the knife. Caspian jumps down from a tree and lands beside me. He hands me a heavy backpack which I take between my teeth.

I dip behind a rock, shift, and get myself ready. The humidity from the forest is already stifling, so I'm glad I packed light clothing. I pull on the sleeveless black t-shirt and dark grey pants, followed by hiking boots, then join the guys.

They're all equipped and ready to go. Good timing, too, as some kind of shifter roars in the near distance.

"Right. Now we need to find a flower that grows in stone," I say, leading the way forward. "Easy peasy."

Caspian falls into step with me. "Where are you going?"

I step over a fallen tree. "Heading North. Apparently, when in doubt, that's the direction in which to go."

"Huh." Caspian leans against the tree and hitches a thumb over his shoulder. "Then shouldn't we be going that way?"

"Yes… I was just… doing a little recon," I say, my cheeks heating up all too predictably.

Caspian and the guys chuckle between them as Caspian helps me back over.

"Why don't we leave the tracking to Alaric? His Rivermare nose will sniff out just about anything."

Alaric is all too delighted to take up the role.

I nod at Caspian. "That would be great."

He playfully rubs my hair while Eziel grumbles to Alaric about losing his 'best knife' to the bet. The

Rivermare voices no intention of returning it, and the four of us trudge through the dense, thick forest.

We only stop for refills by a creek. I kneel at the edge and dip my water bottle inside. The guys are already drinking from theirs and refilling by the time I'm finished.

I straighten up and bring the bottle to my lips. A huge bird perched on a branch catches my eye, and I pause in observation. Silver feathers streak its inky-black wings and its eyes are silver, too, with no irises at all. It cocks its head in my direction and caws once at me, then flies off.

"Did you see that?" I turn to the guys and point where the bird flew off. They were already looking at me studying it. "Maybe it was trying to help us."

Although not all of them seem convinced, they do decide to come with me.

"There it is," I say, indicating the tree winding over the path.

The bird flies off the branch, and we once again follow it. There's nothing about this bird that puts me on edge. Alaric takes over tracking it while I drink from my water bottle. I forgot how dehydrated I was.

I slide the cap back on and glance up at the canopy of leaves overhead. Slivers of light flicker through the trees, momentarily blinding me for looking at them too long.

"Here," Alaric calls, waving us over.

Even as my vision still adjusts, I clearly make out Alaric stumbling to steady himself against a rock. I immediately forget the bird and run to his side. He looks at me, his face flushed and his breathing heavy.

"I'm all right," he says, waving at me. That alone puts him off balance. "I'm… alrighty…"

I gently touch his arm and check his eyes. "They're bloodshot." Moving my hand slowly to see if he follows, my heart clenches. "Alaric, did you eat anything?"

He laughs and sways almost drunkenly. "Nooo, 'course not! The only thing... I wanna eat out here —" He leans in to kiss my cheek. "—is you, if ya know what I mean."

Caspian helps him sit on the rock and checks him over as well. "It's like he's pissed out of his head."

"Psssht!" Alaric tries to stand and nearly falls on his back. "I'll drunk the lot of ye under the table."

"As much as I love your Scottish accent coming out," I say, lightly patting his shoulder, "you need to rest."

"It must've been that creek." Eziel lifts up his bottle of water and tips it upside down to show it's empty. "Alaric drank two bottles back at the creek. I finished mine about fifteen minutes ago." He pales a little. "If the water is toxic, I'll become like him, too."

"Fuck!" Caspian kicks up a bunch of dead leaves. "That fucking Terraseeker! He probably set all this up." His face fuming, he drags a hand through his hair, and then tosses his bottle aside. "I only drank half a bottle. I'll search for the flower. The rest of you hide. There were some more abandoned ruins back down—"

Emptying my bottle on the ground, I shake my head. "No, you might get ambushed when your symptoms start to kick in. I'll go. I barely took a few sips."

"*Oooohhh, flower o' Scooootland!*" Alaric screams from the top of his lungs, and points at me. "*When will we seeeeee, yer like again!*"

Caspian sighs and reluctantly nods my way. "Go and we'll watch over the Big Guy." He turns to Eziel. "You better not start singing too, man, or you're on your fucking own."

I hesitate about leaving, worried about the three of them being alone, potentially intoxicated, in the middle of a strange forest. But we need to win this trial. It's not just for my freedom—it's for our future. While Ez and Cas are preoccupied with trying to stabilise Alaric, I sneak away into the shadows of the trees. It's up to me now to win this point.

Wings fluttering through the trees overheard draw my head upward. I squint my eyes against the blindsight, adjusting. "Oh. It's you again."

The bird from before caws and swoops over to a tree much farther away. It waits and watches me.

"All right," I say, adjusting my backpack. "Lead on, my avian friend."

Wiping the beads of perspiration from my temple, I follow my unexpected guide. Other than the faint tingling in my fingers and toes, I don't appear to be suffering from any other symptoms. Probably because I didn't drink much of the poisonous water, thank goodness.

"I don't suppose you know where I can find a flower that grows in stone?" I ask the bird, ducking under a bent tree. "My guys are sick and I need to end this before things get bad."

Another caw and it flies to its next post.

"I'm gonna take that as a yes and that you're helping—"

My words are cut off as I fall through a nest of leaves and into a ditch. Water drenches me, pulling me under. Spitting out the mouthfuls that managed to claw a way inside me, I grab onto all the roots or weeds I can and pull myself out. I'm drenched by the time I reach the surface. While it's refreshing against the heat, I also know I've just made a terrible mistake, and that whatever hopes I had of avoiding the poison are now dead in the ground.

I practically just took a swim in it.

I bend over to catch my breath, and the bird flaps its wings from a nearby branch.

"Please… tell me… you can help," I say between gasps.

The only hope I have to go on is the bird flying away again.

I guess there's only one way to find out if I'm being led to my victory or my doom. I raise my head and carry onward, praying that somewhere, not too far away, a flower awaits.

"Lilith, I'm so proud of you…" My mum's voice whispers in my mind. *"And you've finally come home."*

That voice…

I spin around, squinting my eyes against the sunlight. "Mum?"

My mum appears under the tree where the bird had been sitting. Her long hair flows around her, as does her swan-white dress, and her smile beams on her face like a ray of golden sunlight.

"Well, what are you waiting on, my darling?" She holds out a hand and motions me to follow. "It's time to go home."

She turns and walks away, her dress billowing in the breeze.

Panic surges through me. "No, wait!" I stumble after her, leaves and branches snagging at my clothes. "Mum, don't go... don't leave me again. I'm sorry!"

My vision blurs and my boots feel like they're filled with lead, but I still keep going. Even when old memories come back to haunt me.

"You smell of weakness."

I ignore Rizor and continue following my mum's light.

"You're the reason my mate is dead, and you will pay for it."

"No," I shout back, tripping over a rock. "You betrayed us, Dad. She died because of you!"

I pick myself up and follow the light until it disappears over the trees. Ducking through them, I emerge in front of a large, round rock.

Rock, save me now.

I rub my head as I taste metal in my mouth, chuckling at my own joke.

Wait, blood? I cough on it as the stone moves, shaking out until it stands up. A giant. A stone giant. The monster is made of black stone, covered in cobwebs and dried leaves. Mold grows down the side of its face and every small movement makes a horrid noise even before it opens its mouth and lets out a bellowing scream.

I fall to my knees, the giant spinning in front of my eyes and making ten of them appear and disappear. Again and again. I barely register the thumps of its feet on the ground, the way every footstep of this thing knocks me over until I'm lying on the ground, struggling to stand. The bright sky above me is cloudless until it's not and a silver bird flies straight across my vision. Mum. The giant roars as I sit up, the best I can. The bird is attacking the giant, crawling and pecking at its face before swooping out of the way.

"Get the flower, sweetheart. Save yourself."

I look around, spotting the yellow petalled flower where the giant was sitting. I rush over and grab it quickly before turning around and running through the legs of the giant, barely missing a giant's foot squishing me. I run into the forest, trees scraping against my arms just as I hear a pain filled bird squawk.

My heart jolts and a cry leaves my lips.

Mum!

Once again, she's sacrificed herself for me.

Knowing I have to honor her sacrifice, I rush through the forest, searching for the river and a way to get myself back to my guys. The flower must be the cure—

I stumble down a hill, crying out as my arm snaps and breaks with the landing.

Shit. Shit. Shit.

A sob leaves my lips as I push myself up, looking at the spinning world around me. I have to eat some of the flower, anything, to save myself first. I can't keep searching through the forest while everything is blurry. I'm sweating buckets, and I feel like being sick. Not to mention my broken arm.

I'm dying. Quite literally dying.

The seven flower petals are glowing as I look at them. Wait, four? Two?

I try to reach for them but keep missing.

"Stop, goddess above, stop." Annastasia's voice hushes at me before I see an outline of her in front of me, right before my legs give out and I end up on the floor, giggling to myself. Seconds later a wet petal is shoved harshly into my mouth and a hand shuts my jaw. "Swallow the damn petal, Lilith."

I reach out and run my fingers through her soft hair. "Your hair is like black candy!"

"Lilith!" she growls, and the shock makes me swallow the petal. Near instantly, the fog over my mind stops and the world goes crystal clear. I sit up straight.

"Can we pretend that didn't just happen?"

"Sure, Candy," she sourly replies, offering me a hand to stand.

"I have to hide, but your guys are close. The flower needs to be dipped in the water to work. One petal each, no more or you'll kill them," she warns me, handing the flower back.

"Are you going to get in trouble for helping me?"

"Not if I get out of this forest quickly," she says and shifts, running into the forest and out of sight.

Despite the nagging worry in the back of my mind for Annastasia, my guys need me more right now. I rush after their scents until I come to the area I left them in, pausing at the sight of all three of them buck naked, passed out on the ground. I wish they weren't dying, or I'd take the time to admire their nice asses.

I run to the river, pouring water over the petals before kneeling between Alaric and Caspian first. My arm throbs but my panic over losing them pushes the pain aside, my wolf taking the brunt of the pain for me this time. I shove petals into their mouths and run to Eziel, doing the same before shifting. Once I'm in wolf form, I let out a mighty howl, enough noise to jolt them, and I keep howling until one by one they sit up, looking a little dazed.

"You okay?" Alaric asks me, and I nod. He looks a little sheepish as he turns to Caspian, who is outright red-cheeked. "Did I dance... naked?"

Caspian looks like he'd rather die than answer. "Around the tree? Yes."

"Brother, you did too," Eziel groans. "And I hate that I sang for you both."

Even in wolf form, I shake from laughter before lying down.

Goddess above, I need a nap. Preferably one long enough to avoid attending the upcoming victory ball.

CHAPTER 14

"*D*o you think your dad will bail us out again?" I ask, still yawning despite sleeping for over ten hours. "Maybe we can use another get-out-of-jail-free card. What do you think?"

Caspian laughs as he adjusts his tux in the mirror. "I think you already used that with Rizor."

With an exaggerated sigh, I sump into the armchair beside Alaric. My dress strains from the effort. If silk and velvet could speak, it would've just screamed blue murder in my ear. "Urgh, this… *thing*… is impossible to move in." I attempt to adjust the emerald corset wrapped around my upper body. Nothing budges, not even one of the lace ribbons crisscrossing my back. "I just about punctured a lung trying to sit down. Alaric, you were my witness. You saw how ridiculous this dress I'm wearing is, right?"

I turn large, imploring eyes on him, seeking moral support. I know my complaining is mostly due to being frustrated that I need to attend this ball. But the dress truly is suffocating me.

He dips his head, his expression all serious. "Aye, I saw it." A sexy smirk slides over his mouth. "I also wouldn't mind getting you out of it."

I blush at the comment yet continue fighting my case. "See, Caspian. Even Alaric thinks the dress is ridiculous." I try to loosen one of the ribbons, but I can't even get a finger inside them. "Nope. I've had enough. Show of hands, who thinks I should slip into a dress that does *not* inflict bodily harm?"

Caspian finishes adjusting his dark green bowtie. "Trust me, if I could convince my old man to help us avoid this, I would." He trails his gaze slowly over my body. "And, for what it's worth, songbird, I'd also rather you were out of that dress."

I remove my black lace glove and throw it at him. "You're as much a pervert as Alaric." My lips spread into a grin. "And I secretly like it."

They laugh as Caspian drops into the chair by the fire. At the same moment, Eziel's familiar chuckle creeps into the room. My breath hitches as he pauses in the doorway of the guest chamber. Just like Caspian and Alaric have similarly been forced into wearing, he's dressed in a plain black tux, but he's opted for a green cravat instead of a bowtie.

Gracefully, he saunters over to join us, and a surge of desire rushes through me. Goddess, he's so handsome. They all are. But Eziel looks every bit the prince I met all those months ago. The only thing he's missing is that big fancy throne of his. He stops in front of me and gives his outfit a once over.

"What is it?" He touches his cheek self-consciously. "Have I got something on my face or what?"

Alaric appears and slaps him on the shoulder. "That's not it, brother. You've just got our little lady all hot and bothered, is all." He grins at me and wiggles his eyebrows suggestively. "Pretty sure if you keep looking at her like that she'll burst into flames."

My cheeks turn an even darker shade of red than my hair. "Umm, that is so not what I was thinking, thank you very much."

Totally was.

I grasp the armrests, and with great difficulty, try to get up. Unfortunately, it's not as easy as it was getting down.

On my second attempt, Alaric reaches over to help me.

"No, no. I've got it. Thanks, Alaric."

"You sure?"

I can hear the smirk in his voice. "Yes, I'm sure. Just give me a minute… or an hour."

While they watch in shameless amusement as I tackle the dress for at least five minutes, I finally collapse into a heap of skirts that puff around me.

"Damn thing is like a blowfish," I grumble with a flushed smile.

Laughter carries between them and it makes me smile even harder.

Despite my flushed state I continue my mission to get up. There's just something to be said about a female alpha who can survive the Demon Trials but not this.

"Oh, for fuck's sake!" Left with no other choice but to admit defeat, I fall back into the chair and stare up at my guys pleadingly. "Death by corset is not how I plan on dying. I require assistance, please."

All three of them charge forward to help me.

Eziel elbows his way past them and extends a hand. "Allow me. It's the duty of a prince to rescue damsels in distress, especially one so fiery."

I shake my head with a laugh. "You're beginning to sound just like Knight with all his duty nonsense." While I do let Eziel help me to my feet, as soon as I'm free to stand again, I lightly pat his cheek in (mostly) playful admonishment. "FYI, I'm no damsel in distress, Prince Eziel. I thought you knew that by now."

Before he can utter a reply, Caspian shamelessly offers me his arm, to which I accept. Eziel's response is a sexy laugh that makes me blush harder and look away coyly.

"You're definitely no damsel," he says, taking up the rear with Alaric. "But you are fiery. Most of the alphas downstairs are intimidated by you."

"Asshole alphas intimidated by a halfbreed they so deeply despise?" I crane my neck to slide him a grin. "Now that I can definitely get used to."

He laughs again and this time the others join in. I love that I can joke with them like this—that I can actually be *with* them again. Soon, it won't just be at these silly trial events. We'll be bonded as a pack and then nothing will get in our way. Bonded for eternity. It's a lovely thought.

The door opens and Caspian leads us to the ball-room. A mixture of nerves and excitement build inside me with each step. The guys can no doubt hear my heart pounding away, threatening to take a run and leap out from my chest. It probably would if this damn corset weren't crushing my organs together.

However, my discomfort is all but forgotten when we enter the ballroom. White flowers twined around green vines dangle from the domed ceiling, where a ginormous chandelier hangs—shaped like a tree made entirely of crystals. The same flowers carry throughout the decor. They wind around the marble pillars scattered around the room and the entire air smells of them. It's sharp and earthy, like the rest of the land here.

"Wow…" Caspian takes the word straight out of my mouth. "Impressive. But let's show these Terraseekers how to bust some real moves."

He drags me onto the dance floor where beautiful yet upbeat music plays overhead. I glance back at the others. Alaric moves straight to the buffet while Eziel grabs several champagne flutes. He catches me looking, shrugs, and then laughs when I grin at him. Meanwhile, Caspian places a hand on the small of my waist. He holds my hand with his other, and together we dance, moving smoothly across the dance floor. He's flawless.

"I had no idea you danced," I say.

"Likewise." He smiles. "Who taught you?"

I smile sadly at the memory. "My mum did. I loved it. What about you?"

Caspian glances away, and his facial muscles tense and thrash. Then he looks back and says, "My father made me take classes when I was young. Apparently, you're not a succubus unless you can dance people into your bed."

I snort sarcastically. "Oh, how romantic."

As if us talking about Lord Dyrk summons him, he appears suddenly at our side.

"Mind if I cut in, Son?"

Caspian visibly tenses at the words. "No. Of course not."

Yet he doesn't release me. Even as the next song begins, he doesn't make an attempt to pass me over to his dear old dad, who just waits patiently. Several Terraseekers, including Annastasia, glance at us standing still on the dance floor.

"Thank you, Son. Now if you could release your partner's hand, for it plays quite an important role in this dance."

Sensing Caspian's anger bubbling up to his surface I smile reassuringly at him.

I'll be okay.

Whether or not he receives my silent message, he does let me go in the end. I watch him fall by the sidelines while Lord Dyrk steps into my line of sight.

"Shall we?"

I hesitate fleetingly before taking his hand. I'd much rather be dancing with one of my guys than him.

Lord Dyrk smiles and effortlessly leads in the dance. For several moments, neither of us speak, and the awkward tension grows with each step. The demon lord merely studies me as though I'm an object put on display for his close scrutinisation.

"You are fond of my son, aren't you?" he inquires, finally breaking the tension.

Although his question is personal and I'd rather not answer it, I reply honestly.

"Yes, I am. More than fond, actually."

"So I have gathered." He spins me in time with the music. "I'm very proud of my son's achievements so far." Another spin, quick and effortless. "But I fear he is trying to achieve a task that may see to his undoing."

My stomach clenches at the implication in his voice. "And what task is that, Lord Dyrk?"

"To be worthy of your love." He continues leading, his skill in dancing clearly advanced. "You see, love is not something demons themselves are capable of feeling. It's something we bring out in others. Mortals, especially, as shifters mostly tend to be stronger in resisting our succubus ways. But you…" He pulls me to him, his eyes narrowed slightly in shrewd assessment. "You seem to bring out this emotion in my son. Perhaps it is because he, too, is a halfbreed. I'd hate to think what would happen should you abuse this power you have over him."

I almost stop dancing at the sound of the accusation. "Caspian means everything to me. I'd never abuse or take advantage of him."

Lord Dyrk keeps moving, practically dragging me with him. "Would you swear on that in the name of our Crescent Mother?"

I hold his gaze unwaveringly. "I'd swear on it with my own life. I would never hurt Caspian Hardling. Ever." I step back, copying the raised hand gesture of the women around me, then return to the demon's side. "Would you hurt him?"

"Of course not," he answers immediately. "He's my son."

"Then swear it. Swear in the Crescent Mother's name that you would never hurt him, your own flesh and blood."

It's Lord Dyrk who stops dancing. He stares long and hard at me, clearly affronted by my insinuation. I honestly don't know what's come over me. There's just something about the way the demon lord is looking at me, his very aura, that forced the words from the depths of my being.

He opens his mouth to reply. "I—"

"There you are." Alpha Eldridge appears just as the song ends. He looks me up and down like a rare cut of meat. "You look astonishingly fitting in that dress, Lilith. As the alpha, I'd be honored to have this next dance with you."

I peel my eyes off the demon lord and turn to the alpha. "If you must."

He laughs at what he probably assumes to be a joke. It isn't. I'm only dancing with Eldridge because I'm surrounded by his pack. I don't think rejecting their alpha will work in my favour. At least, not in public. Or until I've defeated him in the trial.

Lord Dyrk catches my gaze briefly. "We shall continue this conversation another time."

Then he pivots and storms off the dance floor, vanishing into the shadows.

Yes, we will, I vow silently, *and if you hurt Caspian, I will kill you.*

"You're distracted, my dear. What is it you're thinking about?"

Eldridge's voice drags my focus back to him. My stomach heaves at endearment. I decide not to reply with 'murder' and pick the first thing I can think of.

"I'm thinking about how I wished I'd visited your pack long ago. It's surprisingly very beautiful."

A dark glint flashes in his piercing emerald eyes. "*Surprisingly* beautiful?"

Realising my error, I hurriedly try to explain while fighting the blush trying to claim my cheeks.

"What I mean to say is that your pack has always been, err, quite secluded. I had no idea you lived in such…"

"Lilith." He leans in to whisper in my ear. "I am toying with you." When he pulls back, he's smiling, and it *almost* looks real. "I may be a wolf of few words but I'm still capable of a joke every now and again."

I force a laugh and scan the room for an escape.

"Let's go for a little walk," Eldridge says suddenly.

Panicked at the idea of being alone with him, I search for my guys. "I'd rather stay inside, if it's all the same to you."

I can't see them. Where the hell are they?

Eldridge's grip on my waist tightens in warning. I freeze under the pressure and quickly assess my options. I'd like to hit him, very much, but there's too many witnesses. Rejecting the Terraseeker alpha in front of his pack is one thing. Punching him is another. Maybe if I get him alone, I can find out what his motives are. Would he take my rejection easily? Here's hoping.

"Actually, some fresh air would be nice. It is a little hot in here."

He smiles and practically drags me across the room. The open balcony leads out into a private, secluded garden. Hedges and flowerbeds line the walkways and the lamps are few and far between. An instinctive urge to fight or flee grips hold of me. Thank the goddess I managed to hide a dagger in this stupid dress.

"This is far enough," I say, letting my hand fall by my side, my fingers brushing the dagger on my thigh. "Why did you bring me out here, Alpha Eldridge?"

He side-eyes me. "Is it not obvious?" Despite my reluctance, he drags me toward a white pavilion shrouded in gold leaves. "I wanted to get you alone."

I root to the spot and prepare to reach through the skirts for my weapon.

"No need to look so frightened," he says softly.

Wow. If only he knew I was deciding on which part of him to dismember first if he touches me.

"I am *not* frightened," I grit out.

"Aren't you?" He tries leading me into the pavilion, but I dig my heels into the grass, forcing him to look at me. "Why, then, do you disobey me if not out of fear?"

My wolf bristles, urging me to shift and fight him. The fact that the people I care about most are still inside his ballroom, surrounded by his pack, holds me at bay. I need to handle this situation very carefully. I need to get him to back off before things get really ugly.

"What do you want, Alpha Eldridge?"

This time, he doesn't try to force me into the pavilion.

He turns to me, the moon bleeding over his deceptively handsome features. "To pick up where we left off. You owe me after all the help I gave you during the trial."

My blood boils in indignation. "I don't owe you anything, especially not when you *offered* to help me."

A strangely demonic smile lights up his face. "It's this tenacity of yours that needs checking. Although I applauded how you rejected Rizor, in front of his own pack no less, here, in *my* pack, she-wolves obey their alpha. Always." He closes the small distance between us and slides his fingers up my arm, making my skin crawl again. "You'd be wise to obey me, Lilith."

Despite every fibre of my being screaming for me to punch him in the throat, I resort to a different tactic, one I think will work on him and require no bloodshed.

After all, seduction is the perfect bait for predators like him.

I take a breath and pull on my sweetest, most submissive smile. "I do want to obey you, Alpha Eldridge. It's just... difficult for me. I don't know how to obey an alpha as powerful as yourself."

His pupils dilate with lust. "Then let me teach you. Come here, pet."

He doesn't really give me a choice in the matter.

As soon as his lips hover over mine and he closes his eyes, I pull back and stare up into his face.

"You are unworthy of anyone's obedience, Alpha Eldridge, least of all mine."

He opens his eyes, clearly surprised, but does not pull back. He just smiles at me. "And how did you come up with such a poor, inaccurate opinion of me? Do tell, Alpha Thornblood."

He spits my name out as though it's venom on his tongue. Good. It means I'm getting to him. The veins pulsing in his neck and temple just fuel me even more.

"It's not an opinion. It's a fact. You see, I despise men like you. You think that we women—no, *mates*—exist only to obey and do whatever their alpha tells them to do. But you're wrong, and do you know what I'm going to do when I've got my own pack?" I lean in, bringing myself so close that his breath touches my cheeks. "Destroy every-thing. Your stupid, patriarchal rules, or as you call them, traditions, will crumble at your feet. So enjoy all this while you can, because once I win the trials, it's over for wolves like you. I'll make damn sure of it."

He scoffs, his expression twisted in sheer and utter rage, but then a strange calmness comes over him. The smile that spreads over his thinly pressed lips is more chilling than any look or touch he's given me.

"You're right. I should enjoy this while I can." He slowly, deliberately, reaches for his tie and begins to loosen it. "I'm going to enjoy *you*, Lilith Thornblood, and then you'll have no choice but to become my mate. To obey me, as you so put it. My, how we do think alike. I'm going to enjoy you very much, even if you are a halfbreed."

In the second it takes for him to throw the tie to the floor, I lunge for him.

My fist collides with his face, bursting his nose, and I thrust a knee into his groin with every ounce of strength I possess. He doubles over in pain, and I seize the moment to reach under my skirts for the blade. I've barely touched it when he grabs the front of my dress, tears it like wet paper, and slaps me so hard that I stumble back into the pavilion.

Dazed by the rapid swelling of my face and the tears springing to my eyes, I brace myself against the building and tighten my grip on my knife. Eldridge prowls forward like a predator cornering its prey. Or so he'd like to believe. To me, he just looks even more pathetic. He just broke his vow, to The Mother herself, by hurting me. I'd hate to be him when The Mother who gave him all his power takes it back. She is known for being revengeful.

"Has anyone ever told you that you hit like a grandma?"

He just smiles in that sadistic way of his and keeps walking, his shadow stretching over me. "How foolish you are, little halfbreed. Tonight could have gone so much better for you, Lilith, if you'd only obeyed me." He glances at my torn dress and the searing handprint no doubt burning on my cheek. "Now look at what you've made me do."

My revulsion takes over, and I spit at him like he's the most disgusting creature to ever walk the universe. A droplet of my bloody saliva lands on his white shirt. His features twist into something dark and sinister when he looks at it, but then he stills and breathes in the air, his nostrils flaring. His eyes widen in alarm as three scents I know all too well gather around me, forming some kind of protective shield.

"Oh, Eldridge. Now look at what you've made my guys do," I sneer, smirking at the alpha now cowering before me. "My, how I'm going to enjoy watching them rip you into pieces."

By the time my guys appear, Eldridge has shifted into his wolf. He retreats into the shadows and runs back to his home.

Coward.

Caspian is first to reach the pavilion. He sweeps his eyes over me and the blood drains from his face.

"What. Happened?"

"N-nothing," I stammer out, just as Alaric and Eziel stop beside me. They, too, take me in with pale expressions. "Honestly, I'm fine. It just turns out Alpha Eldridge is a disgusting beast who thought I owed him for helping me in the trial.

He got a little handsy but look, he only managed to tear my dress a little. Besides, I had my trusty sidekick with me."

I lift my dagger, the one Alaric gave me, and try to give them a reassuring smile. All three of them stare at me and then each other. Their shock gives way to complete and utter fury.

"I'll kill him,`" Alaric bellows. "I'll fucking kill him with my bare hands!"

"Already one step ahead of you, mate." Caspian withdraws a knife from his coat pocket; the red blade crackles with dark, demonic magic. "Let's go."

"No, you can't!" I grab the two of them before they storm off and make matters worse. "You can't go in there."

Alaric's features contort into a dangerous scowl. "He tried to take advantage of you, Lilith. That bastard needs to be punished."

"And he will be in time," I say, my hands strangely trembling as I hold on to them. "But killing an alpha in his own territory isn't the way to do that. It'll just make things worse and even more wolves will hunt us in the last trial. That's not what either of us need right now."

Eziel softly, comfortingly, rubs my back. "Tell us what *you* need, Lil. Say it and it's yours."

I look up at each of my guys and a strange need to be held by them overcomes me. Maybe it's the shock from what happened kicking in, or the adrenaline still coursing through me.

"All I'll ever need in this world is you three."

As the words leave my lips, they close their arms around me, and I breathe a sigh of relief. I've never felt as safe as I do when I'm with them like this.

This wolf, this prince, and this half demon are the ones I choose to be with. *They* are my mates.

And I will always, and only ever be, their mate.

CHAPTER 15

"I think you're going to love the Rivermare pack," I softly tell Dragon as I gently place her into my shoulder bag, where she curls up in the green blanket she has fallen in love with from this pack. It's the only good thing we are taking from here, and if I never come here again, it wouldn't be soon enough. Knight jumps in after her, looking less convinced in a strange blue tutu that looks like it came off a Yoga Ken doll.

He huffs. "Their alpha is Alaric... I'm not impressed."

"No one can say he isn't honest," Alaric groans from near the door. "Brutally honest."

"I have something for you. From us both," Knight says, like he can't hear Alaric, and I try not to giggle. I look down as Knight holds up a green ring. The ring is beautiful, an emerald encased in silver and shaped like a dragon.

"That looks expensive," I say, sliding the ring on. "Please say you stole it from Alpha Eldridge?"

"Yes, I did. It was hidden with several security alarms protecting it. It was fun to break them all," he brags. "I also made sure his cash reserves are nothing more than ash now."

"Knight, you're a genius!" I exclaim.

"Duh," he replies as Alaric bursts into laughter and Knight glares at him. "Don't laugh at me, Wolf Viking."

I chuckle and zip the bag up, shaking my head at the pair of them. "I think you both secretly love each other and that's what's going on here."

Alaric looks at me strangely, making me pause. His sea-blue eyes search mine for a long moment, and we are interrupted by a knock at the door. Alaric clears his throat and pulls it open to Annastasia, who bows her head. Her eye is black from bruises, from a punch if I had to guess, and her lip is cut, dripping blood down her chin. Blood covers her right arm where it looks like something is written and her clothes are torn in several places. I rush to her as she falls into Alaric's waiting arms. He picks her up and carefully places her on the sofa. She smells wrong in so many ways, and I reach for a blanket, covering her up. I don't know what happened to her, but it doesn't scent good. Alaric meets my gaze, and neither of us needs to say a word. We aren't leaving her.

"Alpha Thornblood, I want to join your pack. I c-can't stay here," she pleads with me, reaching for my hand. I take her hand, hearing the portal being opened in the room. "Please."

"I don't have anything to offer you but my name, my protection, and a place in the pack I will create," I say, clutching her hand tightly in mine, remembering the words alphas say to new wolves joining their pack. "I welcome you to my pack, Annastasia. My blood is yours and by my soul, Mother above, I will protect you."

A warmness fills my chest, spreading throughout my body and down to my hand clutched in Annastasia's hand. My hand glows, the four rings

I wear feel like they are painlessly burning my skin. I turn away as the light becomes so intense it's impossible to look at, and a voice fills my mind.

"Thornblood pack Alpha Lilith, you have been chosen. I honour you with my gift. Save the world, my child. Save and protect my wolves."

Tears fill my eyes as I open them and feel a lump in my hand as I pull it away from Annastasia's grip. There, in my palm, is an alpha's stone given to me by the Mother. She was here. My stone... I'm a real alpha now. I have a pack. The Thornblood pack. It's a mixture of each of the rings, four colours divided in sections to make the diamond shaped stone. It glows brightly with each colour, white, blue, green, and red.

I look up at the ceiling, closing my eyes. "I promise, on my life, to save your wolves. Thank you, Mother."

Further than that, I feel Annastasia bond to my pack in my mind, like a tether I can reach out and tug if I want to. Connected. She is in my pack.

"Alpha Thornblood." Alaric bows his head at me, looking proud. "It's an honour to witness your beginning."

"She was here. The Mother," I whisper around a sob. "She gave me an alpha stone."

He grins, and I turn to Annastasia, who has passed out. "We need to get her to a healer."

"Yes," Alaric says, coming over and picking her up. "Go through."

I walk through the portal and into the meeting room where the betas and Eulah are waiting. Eulah's eyes widen when she looks at me and she goes to her knees, as do the betas, until the room is bowing. "A new alpha is a blessing to the world."

Alaric walks through the portal after me, and I rush over to Denzel. "One of my pack members is hurt. Will you heal her?"

"Of course, alpha—"

"Thornblood. But everyone in this room can call me Lilith," I say as Alaric walks over.

"Take her to the pools," Denzel calls, rushing to Alaric and placing his hand on Annastasia's cheek. His eyes sharpen with anger. "Immediately."

I follow them, Eulah coming with us as we go to the top floors. Alaric places Annastasia in the water and Denzel immediately starts using his power as I watch impotently from the door, unable to do much.

"Go with Alaric. I will stay to help Denzel and heal her as much as I can," Eulah softly tells me, placing her hand on my arm. My alpha stone glows in my hand, and I nod, knowing she is right and there is nothing I can do right now. Alaric walks over to me and wraps his arm around my shoulders, guiding me out of the room and down the corridors.

"Do you think she will be okay?" I ask him after a pause.

He looks me in the eye. "It's an alpha's job to make sure everyone is okay, or at least it should be. You gave her a home and protection. My healer will not let you down."

"Denzel is goddess sent," I reply.

He smiles before he kisses the side of my head. "Agreed. I want to show you something."

"Okay," I say. We head out through the pack and down the gardens at the side of the castle, following a stone path into a thick forest of trees that cut the lights out, making it dark and hazy. My bag rustles, and I open it, pausing to let Dragon and Knight climb onto the thick grass, the smell of water mixing in with the musky scent of the forest.

"Let's explore!" Knight exclaims, jumping and running up the nearest tree, disappearing into the branches. Dragon lets out a sweet, excited noise before flying up and through the trees after her friend.

"They love it here, and they've not even seen the best bit," I say, going back to Alaric. He wraps his arm around my waist as I lean into him.

"Which is?"

"The lake, the mountains, the ocean. I really do love your pack lands. I can see why you kept them away from the world."

"Humans ruin anything beautiful and try to warp it into something more rather than enjoying what it is. Wolves, as it is our nature, try to own and control what we see as ours. This land might be mine in name and title, but it belongs to the Mother. I am her keeper," he tells me, pushing away some bushes in our path before I walk ahead of him. "I believe all alphas are keepers of this world."

"I love that way of thinking," I admit, running my fingertips across some nearby leaves. "The Mother has been so close in my life."

I pause, holding up the stone I haven't let go of. "She gives us paths through life, but it is her who gave us life. We are hers."

"It really is beautiful," he tells me, his eyes looking at the stone. "Many alphas will not like that your stone represents all four packs, creating a new one, but I personally love it."

That word again.

"I really need to put it down," I chuckle, sliding it into my bag and doing the zip up.

"You can't lose it and it cannot be stolen," he tells me as we carry on down the path, and I start to hear water tip tapping against rock. "The stone is bound to you with magic. You can close your eyes and it will come back into your hand."

"That's good to hear."

Alaric pauses and lifts back a curtain of vines to reveal a small cavern tunnel with light pouring from the other side, the water sound coming from in there. "After you."

I smile at him before walking into the cavern and through to the other end, pausing at the incredible sight. Water pours in from a large gap, onto hundreds of tiny, floating rocks that hover in the air above the cave. The droplets that fall from the rocks make it look like it's constantly raining and the floor of the cavern is covered in white, red, green, and blue flowers of all types and sizes.

"I was drawn here when I was young. No one else could ever walk in," he softly says.

"No one?" I question, tears filling my eyes at the sight of this place.

Alaric stops at my side. "No one. When I saw that stone of yours, I knew why. This place is yours, and I was shown it in order to show you. The Mother wanted you to come here."

"With you," I say, taking a step into the flowers, the warm water raining down on me. I walk backwards, letting my bag slowly drop to the ground. "You're my mate, aren't you?"

"Yes," he says simply, directly, perfectly. No lies. No hesitation.

"I love you, Alpha Lyulf Alaric of Rivermare. I have been in love with you since Japan, and I have felt connected to you since before even then. You saved my life, showed me patience and kindness I didn't know I needed or even deserved. I might be a little complicated, and I have a fight ahead of me... but if you let me, I will be at your side. I will fight for the chance to love you. I want you. I want a future with you."

The water is the only noise as I stop breathing, waiting for his response. I've never spoken directly from my heart like that, knowing full well he could reject me.

I've been rejected before, but not by Alaric. Not by someone I love.

Because I do love him. I love him so much it hurts with every breath I take to not scream it from the rooftops.

Alaric slowly smiles, taking large steps until he is in front of me. His lips crash into mine as he cups my face, and I moan from the feel of his lips, his hard body pressing into mine with every brush of his lips. He doesn't pause, taking my lips hard and faster with every second.

"I love you, Alpha Lilith of The Thornblood pack," he murmurs between kisses, branding the words to my lips. To my soul. "Be my mate when these trials are over. Be mine."

"Yes," I say, my heart filling with joy.

He grins as he lays me down on the flowerbed, covering my body with his. Our clothes are soaking wet as we rip them off, desperate to have more of each other. His hard cock soon presses into my core, and I gasp as he plunges into me, my nails digging into his shoulders. He is huge and wide, stretching and filling me in a way I didn't know I could be filled.

"Fuck, you feel—"

He pauses in a pleasure filled growl, his eyes flickering with blue magic.

Using all my strength, I flip us over until I'm on top and roll my hips, enjoying the power I have as I ride him. He rubs my clit with his thumb as I go faster, my eyes locked onto his with every single movement, moans escaping my mouth. I cry out as I intensively orgasm, tightening around his cock. He flips us one more time and thrusts harder, faster, before spilling into me with a long, possessive growl.

Running my hand through his wet hair, he lies on my chest, holding his weight with his arms. His voice is gruff, filled with desire. "We aren't leaving here until I hear you make that noise when you come at least ten more times."

He kisses his way down my chest. "Ten times? I mean I'm not going to complain but—"

His tongue makes me stop talking and thank the stars above for this alpha.

For my mate.

CHAPTER 16

"Something is off...," I say to Dragon, as a salty sea breeze blows in through the window, carrying with it the noise from the city.

She blinks her eyes open and stares at me from my other pillow. *"I feel it as well. The last trial is today, and the world is tense,"* she replies. *"I will be close, in the water."*

"Thank you," I say, climbing out of bed. "I should warn Alaric."

Knight jumps out of bed with me and follows me around my room as I get changed. I quickly shove some snacks into my mouth as I pull my boots on. To finish, I braid my hair tightly, not needing it in the way for today. Not if the nagging feeling in my chest is right and something is wrong.

"Coming?" I ask Dragon and Knight. Dragon flies through the air to my shoulder, curling around my upper arm while Knight takes my other shoulder, holding onto my braid for support. My daggers are strapped to my thighs, and I'm ready for anything.

Today is going to end the trials for... me.

I follow Alaric's scent down the corridors until I find him in the meeting room, sitting on the table, looking at something on his phone.

"Something's not right," I say as I walk in, getting straight to the point. Alaric looks up with a frown, and Eulah leaves the betas to walk over to me. "I sense it. I don't know what is wrong, but something is."

"The seas are stormy," Eulah says when Alaric looks her way. "The future has been clouded since the trials began and I am not sure what it means. I have no one I can ask for advice."

"You did your best, Eulah," Alaric gently says. "I agree something is not right. I woke up late in the night, disturbed by the feeling."

"I don't think we should go today," Eulah states. "We should postpone it."

"We can't do that," Alaric says. "They're all coming and canceling would be an act of war."

"It's better than seeing what storm lies upon the horizon," Eulah protests.

Alaric sighs and turns to me. "What do you think?"

"We cannot cancel this," I agree with him. "Something has warned us and we can all be on guard. We can handle ourselves, and if anything goes wrong, we leave immediately."

"Agreed," Alaric states, his voice final.

"This is madness," Eulah claims, and she isn't wrong; no one disagrees with her. For the next hour we prepare in every way we possibly can for this last trial. So far I'm in the lead two points more than anybody else and we only have to get me one point to win this. Alaric makes it clear that both he

G. BAILEY & SCARLETT SNOW

and Caspian, and likely Eziel will be helping me get a point. It's still risky, and we will need all the help we can get. There's no way this day is ending without a good fight for my freedom and for me to win this. To win my own freedom and my own choice to mate with who I want. Rizor wants me dead. I have no idea what Alpha Mathi wants because I think deep down he is in love with Aurelia. Not that she will ever forgive him. Alpha Eldridge, I know what he wants, and I'd rather die than let him take me as his mate. Death would be a kindness. Alaric. My sweet, Viking wolf who I'm in love with. It should be our choice to mate when we want to, our decision when the time is right and we want to swear to the Mother and take each other as mates in front of the people we love. Dragon and Knight look over at me from the window where they are waiting to sneak into the trial.

"Ready?" Alaric asks, softly touching my back. I look up at him, the alpha who snuck into hell for me and saved me. He saved me. I lean up and kiss him passionately, pouring into my kiss all the words I won't say in front of a room of wolves.

He groans as I lean back, his eyes filled with blistering desire.

"We are continuing that when we get back," he promises.

I chuckle, the amusement and moment lost as Eulah opens a portal into the room.

"Leave," Alaric commands. The betas go through first, then Eulah. I follow through, side by side with Alaric. We step out together at the same time onto the small island in the stormy seas right outside the pack lands of Rivermare.

Eulah was right. The sea is stormy and insane. Waves larger than houses crash against the rocks behind us, spraying us with salt water. This trial is all underwater, thankfully. The rocks in front of us are covered in scuba diving gear, enough for all of us to use.

I know Alaric's chosen this island for a reason, and he has planned everything. He's even decided where we have to jump in, how to get out fast. Where's the best place to get what we need and get out quickly if any sea monsters are about.

Which, according to Alaric, is highly likely in this area. He had to pick a dangerous place, where it was a risk for us all. We have to pray the Mother is on our side like she was in Caeli. Slowly, portals appear around the island, right on time. Alpha Eldridge turns up first, and I glare at him, wanting to let my wolf free to kill the bastard. Alpha Mathi and Alpha Rizor step out next, followed by Caspian and Eziel last. We wait in silence, other than Rizor tapping his foot and the crashing noise of the sea, for Lord Dyrk to show his face.

"Where's your father, halfbreed boy?" Rizor growls at Caspian.

Caspian glances at me, gritting his teeth, then back at Rizor. "No fucking idea."

The Stormfire alpha scoffs. "I'm not waiting all day in this hell sea."

"Then we will wait for him," Alaric states.

Rizor bares his teeth but Alaric growls right back.

So… this is fun.

"It's ridiculous he's even in this trial. He's a demon," Alpha Eldridge states.

"It's not ridiculous," Caspian counters. "Once, Demon Lords ruled this world… until alphas showed up."

"That sounds a lot like treason to the Mother," Alpha Eldridge growls.

"It's the truth, and the world was fine. My father is a demon lord, and he isn't a monster. He is your equal in power," Caspian replies.

The moments feel more tense with every passing second as Alpha Eldridge and Caspian stare each other down.

"Something is—" Eulah manages to say just before I sense it. The thick, dark magic appears in the surrounding air. The island starts to rapidly shake under our feet, large cracks appearing in the rock. I harshly slam onto the ground and Alaric falls next to me, rolling to catch my head and pull me into his arms to protect me. I look up to see Eziel thrown into the sea as the rock under his feet disappears.

"Eziel!" I scream, my voice lost in the chaos. He has to be okay. I sink my head back into Alaric's shoulder, praying that this will pass soon. The shaking slowly stops, the smell of ash and dark magic lingering in the air.

Alaric looks up at me as I lift my head. "We all need to get out of here. Now."

I don't bother agreeing with him out loud as we stand up, and I look over at Rizor, who is the only one standing on what is left of the island, broken into several large pieces. I glance around quickly, spotting Caspian on the ground, too far for me to get to him.

Rizor opens his mouth to shout, but he pauses as something appears behind him, something made of lava and spitting fire in every direction. It crawls out of the gap in the rock like a snake and fear curls around me. It doesn't have a head, just carved out eyes in two large bones and sharp bone claws stretching from its stomach.

"What is that?" I whisper as Alaric pulls me closer.

"I have no fucking idea," he replies as it slams one of its claws straight into Rizor's shoulder. Rizor roars, shifting straight away and sliding himself off the claw.

I turn just in time to see Alpha Eldridge stand up and gasp as a claw slices through his body from another one of the creatures, killing him instantly.

I can't even feel bad for him.

But I don't want to fight these things.

"Get out of here!" Alpha Mathi shouts, running across the space between us. It's only us on the rocks, Eulah and the betas must be in the water with Eziel and there is nothing we can do as one of those creatures rips Alpha Mathi's head off his shoulders and it rolls into the gaps.

"I'm going to shift, and we can swim out of here," Alaric says just before shifting into his wolf. He stands in front of me. I pull out my daggers as Caspian lifts his head and I take a step towards him.

"Cas!" I shout, drawing the attention of the monsters.

They don't look Caspian's way as he pulls himself up and runs for me, dodging the fire bodies of the creatures as Rizor fights one of them.

Caspian just gets to us when the demon monsters stop and a portal opens in the middle of them. He takes my hand, looking at me once. Rizor is bleeding on the ground and the other alphas' bodies are being burnt from the heat of the creatures. I try not to think about Eziel and Eulah in the sea.

Lord Dyrk steps out of the portal, dressed in a red tux with a psychotic smile.

"Now two of the alphas are out of the way, let's finish the final two and take over the world." He holds out a hand. "Shall we, Lilith?"

"Are you insane?" I ask. "I'm not going to help you kill them!"

He tuts. "But you are an alpha. Yes I sense it, even if these idiots haven't looked closely at you. The Mother leaves a reek of power on anyone she blesses."

"How did you master those monsters? Where are they from?" Alaric questions.

Lord Dyrk looks over at Rizor. "Rizor locked them away and left me with the keys. Idiot. Now they want the world back, and I am their way of getting it. They obey me."

"So I guess the important question is, what do you want?"

"I need your power, Lilith," he says. "Come with me and I will spare the Rivermare pack and everyone left alive on this island."

"And if I don't?"

I feel his answer before he says it. "They die and you come with me anyway. I don't need you to be conscious to use your power."

"*Nooo!*" Alaric roars, shaking with anger as he shifts back, grabbing my shoulders.

I turn and look up at him, my alpha stone burning in my pocket. I glance at Caspian and think of Eziel and Eulah in the sea who need help. We have been backed into a corner.

"I have to go with him," I softly tell Alaric.

Caspian turns to me, his eyes burning with anger before he turns to his father. "Would you kill me? Because you're going to have to. You will need to kill me to get to her. And, trust me, Father. I won't be an easy win."

He laughs before grinning. Out of nowhere, the ground under our feet gives way, and I gasp as I crash into cold water. I open my eyes, freezing from head to toe, and there in the water appears a fire portal. I barely get to scream before I'm pulled through the portal and I roll over the ash covered floor, coughing on water. I lean up, blinking through the water to see Lord Dyrk close the portal with a snap of his fingers.

"I guess I won the trials. Welcome home, my alpha female." His lips twist in a sinister grin. "I look forward to our mating."

EPILOGUE

DOVE

I wake up with groggy eyes, blinking several times as light pours in from a nearby window, soft and gentle. So unlike the pits of Hell or the freshness of the bitter air of the Terraseeker pack. A hand rests on my shoulder, and I turn to see my sister sitting next to me. Shock makes my body shake, my wolf howling in my mind as I reach out to touch her pale cheek. My sister, with her bright red hair the same colour as mine, is here.

Wren.

I haven't seen her in so many years, so many that I'm not sure she is even real. Wren is so thin, her cheekbones sticking out and sharp, her face marked with tiny scars, and the blue tee shirt with an England flag on it hangs from her shoulders. My sister's eyes meet mine, and I sob as I see the horrors in her eyes, the pain she must have been through. The prisons are monstrous places, and she has been kept there for three long years. My only sister. The one I was meant to protect.

"How?" I whisper. "Am I dreaming?"

"Prince Eziel got me out, and Caspian took me from the Stormfire pack. I'm real," she says and jumps into my arms. "I know you tried to save me. I'm so sorry and thankful for you."

I wrap my arms around her as I burst into tears. "I did something terrible. I betrayed my friends to save you. To get you back from Rizor, and I can't fix what I did."

"I know," she says, pulling back. "I have this note from Caspian. It was addressed to us both. Can I read it?"

"Yes," I say, needing to understand why I'm here with my sister. Why Caspian would help me at all after what I did to him and Lilith.

Dear Dove and Wren,

We all grew up together, which seems so long ago, and I will always be thankful for your friendship through the dark times in my life. I wish to the Mother you came to me when Wren was taken, Dove, and I would have helped you rather than watch the deal you made with Rizor hurt us all. I'm angry with you, and maybe I will be for a long time, but Wren is too kind to be locked away. Protect her. Lilith and I have spoken, and she wishes you to know she understands what you did.

But you still deserved to be punched, so she isn't sorry about that.

In the bag under the bed is money and new IDs. Hide for a while with the humans, and when everything settles, Lilith and I will come for you both to find you a pack. As you know, the pack world is changing, and I believe a new pack will be born from this chaos.

Be free, and know you are forgiven.

With my love,
Caspian Hardling.

I smile before breaking into tears, feeling completely undeserving of their forgiveness. Wren wraps her arms around me and holds me tightly for a long time, until the ground starts to shake. The shaking continues as I stand up off the bed and walk to the window, looking down at a large bridge outside hanging over a river, filled with cars and a red bus which stands out.

"Are we in London? That's Big Ben, right?" Wren says as I look up in time to see Big Ben smashed into pieces and hot lava shoot up out of the space where it was, pouring into the streets below. Human screams fill my ears, and I watch as a demon monster with eight legs, a goat bone head and glowing orange eyes crawls out of the lava.

"What the hell is that?"

Wren stares unblinkingly at the chaos spreading around us. "It's Hell on Earth... The ancient demon monsters have finally been set free. May the Crescent Mother help us all because the world is going to burn."

. . .

READ THE NEXT BOOK BY CLICKING HERE...

G. BAILEY

G. Bailey is a USA Today and International Bestselling Author of fantasy and paranormal romance.

She lives in England with her cheeky children, her gorgeous (and slightly mad) golden retrievers and her teenage sweetheart turned husband.

She loves cups of tea.

Chocolate and Harry Potter marathons are her jam and she owns way too many notebooks and random pens.

BOOKS BY THIS AUTHOR:

HER GUARDIANS SERIES
HER FATE SERIES
PROTECTED BY DRAGONS SERIES
LOST TIME ACADEMY SERIES
THE DEMON ACADEMY SERIES
DARK ANGEL ACADEMY SERIES

SHADOWBORN ACADEMY SERIES
FALL MOUNTAIN SHIFTERS SERIES
THE REJECTED MATE SERIES
THE EVERLASTING CURSE SERIES
ROYAL REAPER ACADEMY SERIES
DARK FAE PARANORMAL PRISON SERIES
SAVED BY PIRATES SERIES
THE MARKED SERIES
THE ALPHA BROTHERS SERIES
A DEMON'S FALL SERIES
THE FAMILIAR EMPIRE SERIES
FROM THE STARS SERIES
THE FOREST PACK SERIES
THE SECRET GODS PRISON SERIES
CONSEQUENCE.

OTHER PEN NAMES:

LOUISE ROSE & VIVIAN STAR.

SCARLETT SNOW

Scarlett Snow comes from a big family in a small Scottish town and has always strived to prove that if you are passionate about something, no one can stop you from chasing your dreams.

BOOKS BY THIS AUTHOR:

SHADOWBORN ACADEMY 1-3
SHADOWBORN PRISON 1-3
EVERAFTER ACADEMY 1-3
BEAUTY'S WOLVES
GRIMM
SAPHYRE
ALPHA HELL
THE QUEEN'S PROTECTORS
GHOULS
VILLAINOUS HEARTS
CONSEQUENCE

OTHER PEN NAMES:

KATZE SNOW. KYRA SNOW. NORA WINTERS.

ALSO BY THE AUTHORS...

My fate is in the dark,
And my shadow there is real...

The darkness likes to play in this world.

It also likes to deceive.

In the Enchanted Forest, secrets thrive and one girl desperately needs to find answers before it's too late.

That girl is Corvina Charles, a powerful Shadowborn—a human who touched dark magic and became something else.

Something dangerous.

At the age of eighteen, Corvina and her best friend are swept away to the Shadowborn

Academy, the one place where magic and
darkness coincide.

It's also where pupils go missing, teachers don't
play by any rules, the therapist is hot, and boys
with dark magic love to seduce your soul.

With death becoming a game at the academy that
not even the Dark or Light Fae seem capable of
winning, Corvina's love life should *really* be the last
thing on her mind...especially when one of the
boys just so happens to be her teacher!

***Shadowborn Academy is a Dark Reverse
Harem Paranormal Fae Romance for 18+.
In this world, not even the shadows can be
trusted...***

CHAPTER ONE

The moonlight bleeding through the trees create flickering shadows that dance around me. I should be afraid of them like all the other children are, but I'm not. These shadows are safe. They're not like the ones watching me from the treetops, waiting to snatch me off the ground.

No, these shadows are different.

They're my friends.

The faeries hiding in them follow me like they always do when I come into the Enchanted Forest. I can't see them but I can hear them giggling and whispering in my ear. They flick my dark curly hair over my shoulders and play with the ribbons on my light blue dress, then the frills of my white socks with the little bunny rabbits on them. It's their way of saying hello and it makes me giggle as I skip through the forest, humming to the song Mama always sings to me before I go to sleep.

Mama and Papa warned me not to follow these faeries. They said they're not like the rest and I'll be in deep trouble if I ever go out to play after dark. That's when the faeries come out. They sing to children like me and promise us things beyond our wildest dreams, but nobody ever sees them again once they follow the faeries into the forest. Mama said it's because they gobble them up for supper. I don't believe her. I mean, how horrible would that be? I don't think we taste very nice.

Pitch said the real reason the children don't come back is magical.

He told me that they grow wings and go to live with the faeries. He said I can do that, too, once I make my wish. I'm so excited. I can hear him singing to me and I start humming along to his favourite song, the one about the raven and the wishing well. I follow his voice, excited to play with him again and eat snacks and tell each other stories. No one else can see or hear Pitch apart from me and the faeries. Although we're the same age, he doesn't look like any of the boys from my village. He's extremely pale with glowing amber eyes and long ebony hair that sways around him like the shadows do in here. I know he's different and that's why I like him.

That's why I'm following him.

Now that it's my eighth birthday, Pitch is going to let me make a wish in the well he sings about. He says only special humans—the chosen ones—get to make a wish here. Sometimes he says funny things like that and I don't understand him. All I want is a pair of shiny blue shoes, the same ones as my dolly. Pitch says the faeries are going to give me them and then I'll finally have the same outfit as my little dolly.

The faeries guide me to the edge of a clearing which is bright from the moonlight shining down. I wave goodbye to them, even though I can't see where they are, then I continue humming and skipping after Pitch.

I can see him now, sitting on top of the well, and my heart soars as I race through the clearing. Once I reach the well, he lifts me onto the stone with him. It's wide enough that the two of us can stand together without falling into the hole.

"It's time to make your wish," he says, and my stomach fills with butterflies. "Are you ready to be born again?" I don't know what he means by that; I just want the lovely shoes. I nod anyway, and Pitch smiles at me. "Then close your eyes."

When I do this, I hold my breath, too excited to breathe.

My heart feels like it's going to burst out from my chest. I feel dizzy and sick and excited.

"Do you remember what we talked about?" Pitch asks quietly. "What you do once you make your wish? It's very important that you don't forget that part."

"I won't forget," I tell him firmly, peeking through my eyelashes. "Can I say it now? Can I make my wish?"

He giggles and lets go of my hand. "Go on, Corvina. Make your wish and make it count."

I let out an excited squeal, then I scrunch up my little face and think really hard because I don't want to mess this up.

—Hello faeries! Please can I have the same shoes as my dolly? You know, the sparkly blue shoes with the pretty bows on the silver buckles? I would like them very much. Thank you.—

With my wish uttered, I open my eyes. Pitch is gone just like he said he would be and I'm alone on the well. I look down into the tunnel of darkness stretching before me. A loose pebble falls away from the edge and drops into the well. It takes forever to splash through the water at the bottom, and I gulp, my palms turning sweaty against my dress.

For my wish to come true, I need to go down there.

Pitch said he'll be waiting for me and that the faeries will even give me wings so that I don't hurt myself. I'll be just like the other children who followed the faeries into the woods and lived happily ever after. Maybe I'll even be able to see my friends, Bella, and Michael and Agnes.

We'll all be faeries together, like we used to talk about.

I turn around and spread my arms out like wings, smiling at the thought of seeing my friends from school again. Taking a deep breath and holding it in my chest, I close my eyes and fall down into the well, praying that Mama and Papa were wrong about the faeries, and about Pitch, the monster hiding under my bed...

Before I plunge to my death, I wake up with a gasp for air, crutching my thin bedsheets in my hands. Pitch wasn't waiting for me. There was nothing but pain and misery at the bottom of that stupid well and my innocent ass didn't know any better back then.

I fell into magical darkness, and as everyone here tells me, that's when I became a shadowborn.

But that's not the part that haunts me every night in my dreams. Oh, no. It's what happened after the pain and misery—after I drowned in all the magical water, my eight-year-old body absorbing it like it was sugar and I was a starving kid. When my heart started beating again and I opened my eyes, I lay floating on my back as the moon drew closer and closer to me. I remember crying and thinking I had been turned into a bug instead of a faery, but it was just the water healing my shattered bones and floating me up to the surface.

The second my feet touched the earth again, my power exploded and I destroyed everything in a five-mile radius, including all the people in the houses.

Including my parents.

And the only living thing was me, covered in ash, lying on the forest floor as the sun rose into a blood-red sky.

Talk about a birthday to remember.

After that, I was picked up by the Shadow Wardens, protectors of the magical world, and thrown in a shadowborn foster home with all the other children that are like me. Only they didn't kill hundreds of people and not one of them in here see their powers like the curse it really is.

"You having those dreams again?" Sage asks, sitting up on her bed next to me and staring at me, the moonlight highlighting her beige skin, curly pink hair that isn't at all messy even though she just woke up. Sage Millhouse is the only bit of this foster home that I've ever cared about and I'm certain it's the same way for her. We came here on the same day, two scared kids who wanted nothing more than to escape this hellhole and the new powers we have. Sage got her power the way most of the kids here did, by being bitten by a shadow-born in their animal state. One bite is enough to infuse any soul with shadow magic, and all it took for Sage was a bite from a fox in her garden.

The fox was never seen again, and Sage nearly died, only to survive and be taken from her parents to come and live here.

The foster home is full of those stories, and it's the main reason I don't talk about my past.

"Always."

It's all I need to say for Sage to get off her bed and head out of the room. I follow her, the old wooden floorboards creaking under my barefeet with each step. Sage holds the timber door open and we head outside into the garden. The cool air is refreshing for only a second before it's nothing but cold nipping at my skin.

"Ready?" I ask her as I stare up, the darkness and shadows comforting me like they always do.

Sage doesn't reply, though I'm unsurprised as she isn't one for words. That's why I like her. I watch her bright purple eyes as she disappears in a cloud of black smoke. The darkness. It's become a blanket of sorts to people like us. As the blackness fades away, there is nothing more than a hawk sitting on the ground, its lavender eyes staring up at me. I grin as I close my own silver eyes and do the next best thing in the world.

I let the darkness take me, creating me into something more.

Something so much better than I already am.

My body disappears into the darkness but my mind always stays, loving the comfort as I shift into a raven and follow Sage into the skies of Blackpool.

Printed in Great Britain
by Amazon